CB Barrie

I0691558

Only Fate Is Written

A Compendium of Short Stories

Editions Dedicaces

ONLY FATE IS WRITTEN

Published by:
    Editions Dedicaces LLC
    12759 NE Whitaker Way, Suite D833
    Portland, Oregon, 97230
    www.dedicaces.us

Library of Congress Cataloging-in-Publication Data
    Barrie, CB
        Only Fate Is Written /
        by CB Barrie.
        p. cm.
        ISBN-13: 978-1-77076-459-0 (alk. paper)
        ISBN-10: 1-77076-459-3 (alk. paper)

CB Barrie

Only Fate Is Written

Table of Contents

Only Fate Is Written

Evelyn always wondered how it was that even though she was the fraternal twin of her sister Andrea it was her sister who had been gifted with prescience and second sight. Evelyn had no such gift, indeed not even her looks could match Andrea's, and it was Andrea who was always on the arm of a new boyfriend.

Evelyn stood in awe at her sister's ability to predict events or take action prior to something becoming a problem. She hardly appeared to speculate or gamble and yet, as they both reached their late teens, Andrea had made substantial amounts on the stock market. It added significantly to the family coffers and allowed life to continue without the need to work. When their parents both died in the same year, Andrea had declared her right to the estate. And so it was; their parents bequeathment being quite explicit - Andrea was to be the only benefactor. Evelyn had no such expectation, and so she simply bowed to the inevitable and meekly deferred to her sister.

In spite of Andrea's many men friends, the two siblings remained a spinster couple. Even as little girls, Andrea had always dominated the partnership and, as the sisters matured into adulthood, Evelyn became the drudge of the two. It was Evelyn who cooked, Evelyn who cleaned and Evelyn who frequently took the sharp end of her sister's tongue. In truth, it was a deeply malicious and one-sided affair. Andrea saw her sister Evelyn as a non-entity, someone who was empty of ambition, intellectually shallow and easily subjugated. Andrea enjoyed her power and at times humiliated and maligned her sister for the sheer enjoyment of seeing her break down and weep.

"Mother and Father despised you, they were ashamed of you. Dear God, what are you good for?"

"Andrea, must you? I don't believe you. Mother told me..."

"Huh, mother told you! No Evelyn! Mother told me... how weak and demanding you were. How she feared you would end up shaming the family, how father was so proud of me and yet appalled that you had come into the world with your simpering, puerile attitude. I was the one that compensated mother and father for all your disappointment - you are nothing but a parasite, and always will be!"

It was always the same - crushed by her sister's enmity and the mocking lies about her parents, she could only escape in the refuge of her room, consoling herself with her dreams.

As the years passed, and Evelyn watched her sister's social life become increasingly decadent, she began to yearn for some of the things her sister enjoyed. Immoral it might have been, but she was human too, and she began to wonder if she would ever feel the arms of a man who loved her, if under God's skies, there was someone born just for her, who would change everything for the better.

In her naivety she was asking for a miracle; she was hardly ever allowed to leave the house, was never introduced to Andrea's circle of so-called friends, and certainly never had any money to buy things that would make her attractive, or more feminine.

The dream began to instigate resentment.

She carried her resentment the more as Andrea became noisily blatant in her love making in the house, allowing her one night stands to disrupt Evelyn's sleep and daily routine.

Even so, Evelyn slowly learnt survival - to became more patient and more stoic than before. With time, and now hardened to being abused by her sister, she was able to keep her dreams private and her reactions neutral. She was certain that soon, very soon, her saviour would appear.

But as the years slipped by and her dream became weaker and more distant, she held on to it only with desperation and a suppressed sense of despair. There were no men to meet, no one sweeping her off her feet and consequently, no love at first sight.

Andrea was no longer her revered big sister, the one she held in awe. Now she was the door of a trap; a trap which imprisoned her and could never be unlocked unless fate took a hand. But, as Evelyn understood too well, Andrea knew all about fate - she controlled fate, and Evelyn was impotent against her sister's ability to decide the direction of her life.

Occasionally there were special days when they both went into town. Today Andrea was scheduled for a dental appointment and for once Evelyn felt optimistic.

It was unlike anything she had felt for a very long time.

She could not establish the cause of her emotion, but she welcomed the sudden change of mood. Even the taxi ride was pleasant and Andrea was, for once, uncomplaining and silent.

As usual, Evelyn had to kick her heels while Andrea spent time flirting with the dentist. Andrea subsequently made her appearance from the dental surgery as if a crisis had occurred, overriding Evelyn's protests as she insisted they rush to the new Maybush department store to buy Andrea some new underwear. Evelyn instantly knew that their next all-night visitor would be the dentist.

It was as they waited for a break in traffic to allow them to cross over a busy intersection that Andrea seemed to shiver and shrink back.

Andrea's sudden hesitation in crossing the street left Evelyn three steps in front, forcing her to turn and come back.

"What's wrong?" she asked.

Andrea smiled, a wicked and self-satisfied smile.

"The man who would have loved you and married you, and made you happy for the rest of your life, has just passed us in his car. But if you think I am going to tell you who it was, you can think again."

Evelyn found it hard to register what Andrea had said and, for a moment, felt disoriented and lost. Standing on the kerb, facing her sister, she was surrounded by milling crowds and streams of traffic, all of which faded into silence as her mind grappled with what her sister had said.

As she came to realise the implication of her sister's cruel remark, she felt a hardening of her resolve and the upsurge of a bitterness and resentment for all the lost years and vile treatment.

The traffic had begun to move and she slowly inched around

The back of her sister who remained standing at the kerb with just the hint of a mocking smile still on her lips. Turning, so she was back to back with Andrea, she pretended to explore her bag while waiting for the traffic lights to change and the cars to surge forward. As the car engines revved and the impatient drivers inched their cars forward, she searched her conscience for any regret, and found none.

Now she was just in contact with Andrea, noticing a slight tremor from her sister. Arching her back and tensing her muscles, she waited for the cars to accelerate away and, as they did so, gave all her strength to one thrust of her buttocks.

Instantly she was moving, slipping back into the pressing, seething crowd, her mind now determined that no matter what, she would take no more mistreatment from her sister. It was a split second later that she heard the scream of skidding tyres and above it all a long, strangled, shriek.

Intent on identifying the source of the roadside scream the packed crowd were too distracted to notice the diminutive figure of Evelyn as, head down, she carefully manoeuvred through the throngs of people and vanished from sight.

Years later, wealthy and now happily married, Evelyn still wondered how that moment of bitter resentment had been so beneficial and had turned out so well.

Now Andrea sat in a wheelchair, unable to speak or move and completely dependent on aids and nursing staff. After the 'accident', Evelyn had spoken to the lawyers and had Andrea declared *non compos mentis*, thereby assuming control of all the estate. It had taken months of investigation and substantial payments to obtain and then enhance copies of the CCTV footage of the day Evelyn had learned of Andrea's premonition. The angle of view showed mainly the traffic stream and very little of the crowds waiting at the junction. Nevertheless, it required extensive time comparisons with traffic light switching to identify the car that Andrea had seen. Even so, the possibilities were only reduced to four possible cars.

Evelyn had three aborted encounters with drivers who had been at the intersection on that fateful day, but when she contrived an accidental collision with driver number four as he left his work, she knew instantly from his dazzling smile and gentle laugh that her happiness was assured.

Now everything promised a safe and loving life - indeed, she had the life she wanted - except for her sister. Nevertheless, regardless of her contentment she would never forgive Andrea.

Of course, Andrea was still aware of the world around her, but she was a prisoner in her own body. Occasionally Evelyn would visit the sanatorium. She would sit by Andrea's side and reminisce about the times when Andrea had cruelly exploited her and made her feel so worthless and insignificant.

Only her eyes told Evelyn that Andrea wanted to die, that she could foresee the torturous years stretching before her - but Evelyn would gently remind Andrea that regardless of circumstances, Andrea was to live at least the years Evelyn had lost, and that her fate was now in Evelyn's hands.

And yet, one thing still puzzled Evelyn.

On the day she had pushed Andrea off the kerb into the traffic, Andrea had shuddered slightly just after Evelyn had turned round behind her. Had her sister experienced a premonition of her oncoming disaster? If so, why had she made no effort to avoid it?

Could it have been the one thing psychic or sensitive people accepted as predestined and unavoidable - that fate was fate, and there was no escape.

Hair Of The Dog

"It won't do!" my editor screamed at me, "For Christ's sake, don't you know the old adage, 'Dog Bites Man' isn't news, 'Man Bites Dog' is! I don't want stories about divorce cases unless she shoots him, wacks him over the head or somehow hospitalises the bastard."

This was the umpteenth time I'd been on the receiving end of my editors notorious ranting and I had to admit it, I still didn't like it. It was typical, of him to sneer at my journalism or embarrass me about my writing style - particulary in front of colleagues even though I was senior. His already alcohol bloated face seemed to become the more swollen and livid as I stood in front of his desk trying to get another chance to interrupt his explosive displeasure. I'd done my best to be diplomatic about the scoop of a story I had uncovered, but he had deliberately misinterpreted what I had been trying to convey. As he took breath, ready to throw yet more invective in my direction, I raised my hand in the hope of deflecting the oncoming tirade.

"Look chief," I managed to interpose, "it isn't just any divorce you know. I got this right from the horse's mouth and...."

He scowled and ignored my protestation. "Huh, I don't give a damn if the horse was married to your grandfather! What you are trying to report ain't news - get that through your thick skull."

I shrank back, this was always going to be a difficult one and his attitude was making it twenty times more difficult than it should have been.

"But this is news chief, big news. This kind of thing doesn't happen that often and I 'm sure you'd want to know about it."

He almost spat at me. "Are you mad? Divorces are happening by the thousand every day! They're two a penny. Get out of my office and don't come back until you have the equivalent of 'Man Bites Dog' and a conventional divorce case isn't that. This newspaper reports important events, and so far you haven't mentioned anything that's worth reporting."

"Oh, but this case certainly is chief." I said, "The woman that gave me this story was special, you should know her, it was your wife - and, by the way, the divorce papers are in the post - she's going to claim everything you've got. Now, how do you feel about 'Man Bites Dog' - is it more newsworthy than 'Wife Bites Editor?'"

I watched with mounting pleasure as his face changed colour from a blotched and sickly red to an engorged purple, all the while glistening with the instant eruption of sweat droplets. He staggered back, a look of horror and disbelief on his face.

One leg suddenly lost support and he twisted sideways trying to keep upright as his right hand clutched his chest. His lips met in a futile, blubbering damn as saliva dribbled out and both eyeballs seemed ready to explode from their sockets. He suddenly stiffened and for a brief moment was caught in a statue like stance before he lost rigour and slammed onto the floor. It was akin to a whale being beached by a storm - a mountain of flesh that was long past its rightful life.

As I went forward to look at my handiwork, the door of the office opened and I was caught in a hubbub of distressed and anxious voices. Unresisting, I was gently led away from the body, guided through the office door, and

14

offered a chair. I heard hushed voices making sympathetic sounds and gratefully acknowledged the kindness of a hot cup of coffee.

They, of course, thought it was shock that kept me withdrawn and uncommunicative. But I knew otherwise!

Inwardly I was consumed with a sense of relief and pleasure. Now seven years of torment were over - the man that had given me nightmares for all that time was no more. Now I could resume being the journalist I had always shown myself to be, without the constant and unremitting criticism I had endured.

It had taken a long time to contrive an affair with the editor's wife, and even longer to calculate the best way to confront him with it. It was the only way I had of getting back at the pig, yet I had never expected the outcome to turn so perfectly in my favour. Now that it had, it occurred to me that I was second in seniority to the assistant editor; someone who would now become the top man. As I remember, his wife was far from unattractive. What I had done today could, with the right planning, be done again. All I had to do was bide my time - 'Man Bites Dog' had been a good lesson!

Looking For Love!

I didn't realise how hungry I was until I walked into the *Cafe Amore* and was enveloped in a mouth watering atmosphere of coffee, fresh toast and full workers breakfasts.

I sat down at one of the red plastic tables quickly scanning a sticky, ketchup spattered, menu. Pictures, in striking Technicolor, of omelettes, home made soups, lunches for the ravenous, hamburgers and pizzas, all shone out from the plastic coated page. It boasted full, partial and vegetarian breakfasts, all with whatever you wanted, including tasty extras and any kind of hot beverage you could think of.

I was seconds away from getting to my feet - intent on going up to the glass fronted counter and ordering a meal - when she (yes, she!) appeared from nowhere.

"Hello sweetie," she said, giving me a huge smile.

I was halfway up out of my chair and as I sank back into it I viewed a young woman with long blond hair. She was dressed in a red dress over which was tied a smooth and spotless white apron. Each garment was wrapped around a very trim figure.

"Oh - hello". I stammered, "Can I give you my order?"

"No problem." she replied giving me another huge grin and grabbing a small, white leaved, paper pad hung from a waistband by a length of yellow string.

"Er... cheese omelette, french-fries and a side salad please - oh, tea and a fresh orange juice as well." I croaked.

She wrote hastily and then gave me a heart-stopping smile that was mirrored in her eyes - each iris widened like the opening of a deep well. With a theatrical flourish, she ripped the top sheet from her order pad and walked off.

As she did so, I actually felt my heart miss a beat. Was I so hungry that it was affecting my heart rate, or was there something about the waitress that had me smitten? I decided it was both, and looked forward to the pleasure of seeing her again.

When she exited the recessed serving area and came towards me I could tell that this particular establishment was generous to its patrons. The closer she came, the clearer it was from her tense arms that the tray she carried was no lightweight, and even at a distance the tray appeared to be overflowing with food. As she bent towards my table I viewed the top of the tray - the amount in the various dishes being enough to feed an army.

As she set the bowls and plates down on the table I couldn't resist looking into her eyes. Briefly looking up at me, her eyes smiled again and she came closer to me than I had any right to expect.

"*Bon appetite*." she whispered and was instantly gone.

She had laid out the plates and dishes in near perfect order, the salad to the right, the basin of french-fries to the left and the omelette on a pre- warmed silver-serving tray directly in front of me. The tea too came in an expensive silvery white teapot with matching cup and saucer. The cutlery was wrapped in a paper napkin and as I unwrapped the napkin I was presented with gleaming metal, so clean (I chuckled) I could have eaten from it!

I devoured the meal with relish, every mouthful becoming increasingly satisfying. When, at last, I had swallowed the last of it I drank the remainder of the tea; with no little regret that I would have to wait a good length of time to experience it all again. One needed a voracious appetite to appreciate a well-cooked meal, and there was no doubt that what I had just eaten was *cordon bleu* extraordinaire.

As I sat satiated, and feeling at one with the world, she appeared again. "Did you enjoy your meal - would you like some coffee?" she asked as she came to the table.

"Absolutely wonderful...best for a very long time but no coffee thanks." I replied.

"Oh, good," she said, "we aim to please."

She leant forward and began collecting the empty plates and dishes. "When you're ready you can look at the kitchens."

Again, a huge smile.

I was somewhat taken aback by her remark, it was not what I was expecting. The bill presentation yes - a question about who I was, or where I came from perhaps - but not an invitation to see where my meal had been prepared.

I tried to deflect her as gently as possible - she was too attractive to risk offending.

"Very kind of you but I doubt I will be able to move from this seat for a while - that was some meal!"

She gave me another pearl white smile. "So glad you enjoyed it... it's not usual for you people to eat here first. Usually you just stick on a white coat and rubber boots and dive in to see the chef and the kitchens."

I suddenly lost the plot. Why on earth would she believe I might put on a white coat and....?"

It suddenly dawned on me that I was not who she thought I was. However, my past experience in local council affairs quickly determined <u>what</u> she thought I was.

18

To her I was an Environmental Health Officer, expected to inspect and assess the hygiene and food preparation protocols in the kitchen, whereas in reality I was temporarily in the locale for a job interview and simultaneously infatuated by a pretty waitress.

What to do?

If I came clean it would reduce my Casanova status to zero. If I pretended to be what I wasn't, there was a good chance she would eventually find out and I would be equally lost. One chance was left.

"Food Standards Agency actually - I'm waiting for the EHO, he was due here thirty minutes ago. I'm going to give him another ten minutes - if he hasn't arrived here by then you can cancel the inspection because I won't be here to appraise him of some changes in the regulations."

I spoke with as much authority as I could muster and it was clear from her expression that it all sounded plausible. "Oh, right." she said, appearing relieved and less smiley than before.

I decided it was the only chance I was going to get and so I threw caution to the wind and asked her.

"You been very kind to me today - I'd like to reciprocate. Would you like to go out with me sometime...have dinner with me...that is if you aren't already fixed up?"

For a moment she remained unmoving and silent. I hoped the absence of an engagement or wedding ring was in my favour but there was no way of knowing for certain.

I looked expectantly at her and suddenly there was that big smile again.

"Okay - I'd like to. Where and when?"

I look back on that meal with a fondness only surpassed by the memories of a certain waitress; after all, why not? She became the love of my life and we have had many years of happiness. My only regret stems from the fact that meeting her was on same day that I was due to be interviewed for a new job. Instead, I kept my old employment and spent the greater part of my engagement to my lovely waitress secretly applying for other jobs - all in the Food Standards Agency. By the time we were married I was what I said I was, an advisory officer in the FSA.

Pity about the other job - my background allied to financial securities had led me to a city outfit called Baring's Bank working with a guy called Leeson. It was the potential of a substantial salary that attracted me, though I had to admit, I was on my way to that interview with very reluctant feet.

I suppose they all made good without me, though my detachment and lack of interest in corporate and current affairs means I'm hardly ever likely to know if it was a glaring mistake. Still, all things considered I'm in no way disappointed, and every now and again my lovely wife and I have an omelette-based meal at her old *Cafe Amore*. When we do, I ask her to refrain from telling her old colleagues what I (now) do for a living - I've no wish to be invited to scrutinize the kitchens! Likewise, I'm tempted to tell her the whole truthful story about our first meeting, but then again - would it serve any purpose?

If It Ain't Broke!

The sage appeared on the rostrum clothed in white gossamer and holding the sacred staff.

Those standing in the temple, those who had waited for this most blessed moment in the holy calendar, then prostrated themselves before the shrine; as was the way of those sanctified. A brief moment of silence was broken by the rustle from the gowns of many hundreds of disciples, adherents, acolytes and temple initiates as the sage let the staff drop once on to the marble base to signify attention. On cue, hundreds rose from the floor to listen.

His voice was like honey, the voice of wisdom, learning and experience. His voice sang blessings. He allowed the hypnotic cadence of his voice to invite adoration and unyielding faith. It was modulated to convey his love for those in the congregation, to express his conviction that those who now listened were the chosen. Not one word was without its suggestion of righteousness amongst the gathering, nothing in his tone failed to communicate the perfection of faith that he knew was instilled in his flock. They listened intently, and as they hungered for the messages, they came in song - and the people were relieved.

"Harken my children," he intoned, "*Ab initio* - from the beginning - the creation of new things, the birth of new ideas and concepts, new approaches and new philosophies all competing with the old - this is your legacy of peace.

Yet we should remember, rebirth and renaissance means the death of what was, of those things we are used to.

21

We do not supersede the old with the new simply for the sake of it, but because we replace the old with something equally superior, because the new is clearly as good as the old. It is when the new demonstrates the deficiencies of the old, when it makes clear the faults and wrongs of the past, that we change our allegiance from the one to the other. Therefore, we install the new at the death of the old - the substitution of one thing at the demise of another. What was is now gone - because to keep it makes heretics of us all. This is why we gather here tonight - to celebrate the new, to celebrate compromise."

The sage paused, amid a palpable atmosphere of expectation - and all the faithful knew that their devotion to change was as it should be. For the *Festival of Giving* had been the glory of the faith for generations - the moment when all the rigours of religious life were liberated by a new awareness - and by a new reverence.

The sage looked about him and gave the sign of the enlightened - one arm crossed against the other in a cruciform, recognised only by those who had undertaken all the holy orders under the priesthood.

"My children, when you go, let the world know that this day marks the advent of a new beginning."

A voice to the left of the rostrum called out "The enlightened one has spoken - let us obey and begin the Festival."

Immediately, small packages were exchanged from one to another. People turned and turned about, each giving and receiving brightly wrapped packages in a constant and unending exchange. Each package was wrapped many times over and as each exchange took place one of the wrappings was discarded. As the minutes passed there began a slow crescendo of elated voices, all chanting in slow melodic mantra the 'Song of Giving.

These were the successful recipients of the packages - the ones left with the last wrapping on the gift, the happy souls blessed with the reward of some festival food.

Though many were overjoyed - some were disappointed. Festival food was a black, fruit packed recipe whose origins were long forgotten. Few of the disciples could face it with total relish but a small minority found it delicious.

Nevertheless, the song of thanks and renewal sang out as the many voices rewarded by the festival food gave vent to their sense of privilege. Had they known, it was actually a very old song, and like theirs it was once, centuries back, sung at a particular time every year.

Now the time had come for the final ceremony. It was almost midnight and the light panels were dimmed as the congregation fell silent in order to hear the announcement of the New Year's catechism. As always there came the appearance of the 'tree' - the magical illumination of a silver, conifer like, shape - studded with small, brilliantly reflective, balls and bell like ornaments. At its top there was the gleaming shape of a star, itself glowing with inner radiance.

A few of the adherents found it impossible not to exclaim as the tree flared into life and many were gripped with a sense of wonder as several muttered the traditional "*In Nomena Christi. Amen.*" However, though it was said by a good few, no one knew it's meaning; if indeed it actually had one.

After a few moments, the Sage came to the fore on the rostrum. He waited as everyone fell silent. Now his gossamer robe was backlit by the radiant tree that had begun to shimmer with different colours. Now was the crucial time, now was the moment the spirit of probability would determine what the New Year brought. Some were pessimistic, others simply realistic. One or two were indifferent. After all, the cycle was not that long, and whatever the 'new' was going to be, it would only last a year.

Suddenly the ceiling light panels came up to full illumination as the twinkling of the tree froze into a fixed display. The Sage struck down with his staff for the last time, faced the tree, and after a careful examination turned back to his flock.

"The old was Roman Catholic, the new is Russian Orthodox," he announced, "The change of observances will be published at the end of this year."

As two of his attendants took his sides, he was escorted off the rostrum.

Outside the temple, the people were free to discuss the 'new year'. There were a few more days to this one, but they knew that soon their worship and obligations would alter - but fortunately only very slightly.

"Thank the heavens its not Buddhism," one was heard to remark, "I almost starved two years back!"

"Starve!" another interjected, "That's nothing, I'm still half crippled from all that kneeling and prostrating during the Islamic year back in thirty three."

This took the attention of an initiate, "Well its just the way it must be - we've avoided conflict and damnation for almost two centuries and imposing a new creed each year, which we all adhere to, ensures we don't get the religious wars like we once did. Remember, millions died"

A young girl hearing this asked "But how many of these changes can there be, and for how long must it endure and for how long can we endure it?" I've been tutored in mixed theology and comparative religions for two years now and I still can't see if it's rational. My grandmother said she began to dread certain years and she's glad she's too old to be obliged to meet all the observances. Wouldn't it be better if we just had the one faith that everyone accepted?"

24

"What?" remarked a bystander, "And have to go through our whole lives risking our immortal souls by worshiping the deity the wrong way. At least as things are we probably get to worship the right way occasionally - I'd rather that than be praying at the wrong alter all my life. Look at the Romans; they had so many deities they were forever sacrificing to one or another in case they had chosen the wrong one. And anyway, I like the *Festival of Giving*, and since it appears in most of the years, I won't miss the cake too often."

"You could have both if we all agreed on the best faith to have." the girl said.

A few nodded their heads and began a discussion with the girl.

Then an unknown voice shouted, "Heretics - I hear heretics."

Those at the centre of the debate turned to seek out the dissenter.

"Mind your own business!" one of the debaters shouted in the direction of the unknown voice.

"Like hell we will!" came the reply and a large rock arced through the air.

Murphy Was An Optimist

It was a bad morning.

The alarm had faltered and he had nodded off again, only to leap out of bed as overriding panic about being late for work energised his movements.

He shaved hurriedly, patting his face free of blood spots and steeling himself for the self-inflicted torture of slapped on after-shave. Then it happened - just as his tense body and watering eyes had endured the agony of the fragranced firewater, a sudden ear-splitting siren from a smoke alarm signified a stream of black smoke billowing from the kitchen. It also testified to the carbonised toast that was to be his breakfast.

As panic and adrenalin induced a dash from the bathroom to the kitchen, his left slipper rolled off his foot and flipped away, leaving his foot in contact with a freezing stone floor. Diving into the kitchen, he refused to be diverted by his frozen foot and lost slipper and, pivoting about on one leg, he tried to unearth the smoke spawning toast.

Waving his arms, he hoped to clear a path through a choking fog of acrid, smouldering bread; but unable to see clearly, or manoeuvre easily, he missed the power button on the toaster. Instead, his fingers found the front of the searingly hot slice rack, and he distinctly heard flesh sizzle just before the pain hit him.

It was agonizing and he was forced to leap for the sink and open the cold-water tap in order to alleviate the intense torment. As the cold water rapidly and mercifully relieved the burns, he was able to open a window to vent the smoke. Almost simultaneously, he heard the toaster over-temperature switch kick in and shut it down. Moments later the smoke alarm cut out.

Three fingers now carried very large and tender blisters and because he had only one useful hand, he found it virtually impossible to treat them. Getting the first aid box cover off was a trial in itself, but trying to detach the sterile paper wrappings from the adhesive dressings was close to a nightmare. When, after attempting to remove their wrappers his teeth had torn three wrapped dressings to shreds, he learnt to manage the process better. After a frustrating fifteen minutes three large dressings cocooned his burnt fingers - though none of the dressings stuck properly.

He soldiered on, looking forward to at least a fresh cup of tea as he attempted to locate an intermittent bleeping which had became audible immediately after the smoke alarm stopped. And yet it appeared to be the same smoke alarm that was bleeping. He inspected the underside of the smoke detector and noted that the low battery LED was blinking along with an audible alarm - the intermittent bleep.
He concluded that the old battery must have been run down already and was now completely spent due to the alarm operating continually as it had. He had no choice if he was to eliminate the annoying bleep and decided to permanently disable the alarm prior to fitting a new battery.

Reaching up to its location on the ceiling, and hobbling precariously on the one slippered foot, he pulled at the cover with his good left hand. It refused to budge. He stretched up again and caught the lip of the cover with two fingers, which should have released it and exposed the inside. However, he was poorly balanced, and as he exerted a little extra force, all resistance collapsed and the whole alarm came away in a cloud of dust, plaster and retaining screws.

He found himself sitting on his backside covered in powdered detritus. The alarm had hit the floor hard enough to cause all its components to disintegrate. Only the old battery seemed intact.

Frustrated to the point of total distraction, he decided that he was to do nothing more to invite catastrophe. He needed a respite and a nerve-settling cup of tea. Everything else was to be left until a more auspicious time.

Still one-footed, and one-handed, he limped back into the kitchen looking for milk, mug and liquid refreshment.

He placed the milk carton he cautiously liberated from the fridge on the work surface by the teapot cosy. Then, taking care to guard his bad hand and bare foot, he left handedly grabbed at a mug recently cleaned in the dishwasher. As his inexperienced left hand locked on to the mug's handle it slipped away, burying itself under a plastic grill at the back of the washer. Cursing, he reached in again and managed to wrap his hand around the slightly wet body of the mug.

As he lifted it out it slipped from his fingers and dropping to the floor crashed down on the front of his bare left foot. He leapt back involuntarily, bouncing his lower back off the edge of the opposing work surface. His flailing arm attempted to steady his awkward stance but, instead, he instantly felt something cold as his arm first impacted the milk carton. As the milk carton was dislodged it lifted and impacted the teapot. In its turn, the teapot thus moved in unison with the moving milk carton and both teapot and milk carton hit the kitchen floor one behind the other.

The burning hot tea exploded from the teapot and hit both his legs and feet at the same time. It was excruciatingly painful and he froze in shock instantly sucking in breath and letting out a strangled shriek. His whole body went in to spasm and he realised he was helpless to alleviate the torture. Paralysed by the pain his chest froze, stopping him fully vocalising the full extent of his distress.

For what appeared to be a lifetime of pain he remained paralysed but then, almost immediately, a tidal wave of ice-cold milk flowed over his feet and legs, instantly subduing the torture.

The massive volume of air he had taken in for the scream was exhaled with relief - it was as though he had been dropped into the fires of hell and then instantly posted to the artic.

It was not his day, indeed not a day for doing anything until Mr. Murphy had left the building. For a brief few seconds he felt his eyes leak tears. Yes, he thought, sometimes crying over spilt milk is all you can do!

Novum Antiquarum

I never thought that leaving University with a Chemistry degree would take me back to my fathers tanning business. I always had dreams of a research job with a big corporation, spending my days discovering new things and breaking new ground on my way to a Nobel Prize.

As it was, I had only just graduated when my Dad contacted me and asked if I would come home for a while. I was still in the middle of tidying up my CV and composing letters of application for some research vacancies, so I was able to promise a few days at home while I awaited replies to the letters I had already sent out.

On arriving home Mum and Dad and my younger siblings welcomed me with open arms and I felt a sudden sense of guilt for not having seen them more during my undergraduate days.

Still, home I was, and glad of it.

It was on the second day that Dad had a private tête-à-tête with me in his study and he told me that he needed my help desperately. I listened intently as he told me that the tannery had been substantially re-fitted during my absence and that on the face of it the efficiency and productivity should have doubled. My father said this in a dejected way, so I knew that whatever changes had been made was not getting the results he had hoped for. I was right. It seemed that in removing all the old plant and process machinery, and replacing it with new equipment, the output quality of the leather produced had fallen to an abysmal level.

My father had years of experience in the tanning business and knew its processes backwards. Okay, maybe he was no innovator or chemist, he said, but nevertheless what had worked in the past should work now.

But it didn't!

The new hide strippers, soak baths, tanning salts and tanning vats were all contrived from, or with, new reagents, conveyors and equipment but the essential process was the same as it was when he bought the business thirty-five years ago. In effect, nothing but the process capacity had changed. As he told all this to me, I could see an edge of panic coming into his voice. Even to someone as much a novice in business as me, I could see that if the tanning problem wasn't solved soon everyone was going to take a severe financial fall, not least my family. Without hesitation I agreed to investigate the predicament and do everything I could to sort things out.

Truth to tell, I knew very little about tanning chemistry, and it was to my shame that I had been less attentive to the aspects of organic chemistry in my university courses. Nevertheless, I was determined to help my father and his employees - so if it meant a crash course in tanning chemistry, so be it. The rest (I assumed) would be common sense, helped along by the expertise of my fathers long serving staff.

When all was said and done I actually had comparatively little to learn, and I began the obvious analysis of the metallic salt concentrations, vat temperatures, soak periods and so on in the process tanks and vats. Likewise, I attempted to get a comparison with the state of things before refurbishment had taken place.

I checked the quality of earlier hides with current ones, had a full analysis done of the current tanning salts, and analysed the soaking baths looking for contamination. I went over every stage bit by bit in as methodical and systematic way as possible. But nothing showed up either as suspicious or extraordinary.

I could see the my father's demeanour change for the worse as day by day I repeatedly reported no decisive breakthrough. The finished hides came out at about a seventy-thirty ratio. A few passable, most rejected, and none as good as they used to be before the renewal of the plant.

As time wore on I became more and more frustrated. It was clear that everyone was losing faith in my ability to solve the problem and I heard mutterings that there had to be another cause - even the idea of sabotage was raised.

I too had concluded that there had to be another factor involved, but I doubted that sabotage was it. Indeed, there was no way the process could be disrupted secretly. I had introduced a whole range of quality control safeguards so that nothing was done that could not be exposed as a change to the status quo. Everything was so tightly organized that I began to suspect that I had missed the obvious; that it wasn't the process at fault but the procedure. Was it possible that when the new plant had been installed a part of the process had been inadvertently left out, or some machinery dispensed with?

Who would know?

I decided simply to ask the question without assuming anything, and let it lead where it would lead.

I had already made friends with all the plant operatives and I began the next day by simply drawing in each man and starting a casual conversation with him. It took a long time before I had made contact with all the men, and had picked their brains for recollections about how things were before the plant was modernised.

It was when I was talking to one of the men at the tail end of my list that a remark was made that sent a chill down my spine. It seemed that the modernisation had not only increased the plant size but also marginally reduced the workforce. To my amazement I was told that during the short shutdown that had to take place when all the salting and soak vats were being replaced three men had left the workforce.

All three had retired. Of these three, two had been in the hide shaving shop so had little to do directly with the tanning process. However, the third man had been a long time operative on the salting vats. He was well known in the plant for having extensive knowledge and experience about the tanning process, having started in the tannery at the time my father had taken over the business nigh on thirty-five years ago.

I was grabbing at straws I knew, but given my abject failure so far, I had no choice but to call on the absent operative to see if he could help.

He appeared two days later - a pleasant and unassuming man with a ruddy complexion and a deep booming laugh.

I explained the predicament and asked if he would go over the final stages of the process to see if he could identify anything that struck him as wrong or strange. He said he would be pleased to do so and we walked in the general direction of the salting vats, all the time hearing his old accomplices calling out greetings to him.

As we approached the vats he was drawing air into his nostrils and looking about.

I asked him what he was doing. He replied that he was smelling the air; he said he could tell instantly from the process odour if things were wrong and, so he told me, they definitely were.

I was trained never to believe in anything that couldn't be measured or calculated and for a second or two I thought the man was trying to make a fool of me. Then I changed my mind, remembering one of my chemistry lecturers telling us that our noses were excellent analytical instruments and, if it smelled bad, it probably was!

I asked him what he meant by 'wrong'.

He said nothing.

Instead he walked over to the operative standing by one of the salting vats and engaged him in earnest debate. After a few moments, they both turned and spat repeatedly into the vat.

I was agog - unable to fathom out what on earth they were doing.

The two men waved a mutual goodbye and my visitor returned to me.

"No problem now." he said, "It will all smell right in the morning."

Unable to reply anything sensible, I escorted him to the works canteen and ordered him a lunch as a thank you. He was very grateful, but I was half expecting it to be a futile outlay. I was wrong - the next day the whole plant was smiling and the QC people were reporting excellent results.

In the ensuing days I pondered on this again as I watched the salting operatives spitting copiously into the vats.

There it was - the lost factor.

It wasn't what was being done that had undermined the process; rather it was the absence of a seemingly trivial piece of old tanning alchemy.

A subtle factor indeed - spitting into the vats!

My father found it hard to accept when I told him.

Had he been an organic chemist he would have realised that a little saliva enzyme goes a long, long way!

Bee's Knees

My family have always been country folk and we still keep our roots in the rural side of the County. We live and work in a small village just north of a small market town and although the sprawl of urban housing is starting to encroach on us, we still have miles of hills, woodland and fields to shield us from municipal contamination. In fact, we have the good fortune of being in an area of outstanding natural beauty, so it is odds on that we won't get a massive and unsustainable housing development in our locale.

We've had a long history of bee keeping among a good few of the villagers, and the village community are used to seeing nectar gatherers buzzing around in the fine weather. They are lovely little things and seem to know that we aren't a threat - we get very few reports of people being stung.

My story starts early on a dewy and misty September morning, with the chill of the previous night still around and the promise of a long hot day ahead as the sun began to rise into a clearing blue sky.

I had a long list of errands to do - delivering some impressive (but just functional) loudspeakers to a local charity, a visit to the bank to get currency transfer details, buying some paint from the hardware store and finally, a big shop at the town supermarket. I also intended to grace the local car wash to have months of dust and grime stricken from the car.

It was as I started to open the driver's side door that I saw the bee. Her black strips, furry back, smallish eyes and unmistakable pollen baskets made her clearly identifiable as a local worker. It was so common to see them resting or nectar gathering that most of us simply took no notice and got on with what we were doing. However, this bee was different - she was stuck to the upper door trim by moisture that had condensed out of the night air onto the cold metal surface of the car.

I was tempted to help by trying to lift her away, but she was a worker and could sting (if I got it wrong) or be damaged (if I was clumsy).

Instead I decided to simply leave her and let the increasing temperature and the air-stream over the car eliminate the moisture and give the bee a chance to fly away. My first errand meant a drive of three miles and as I arrived at the first stop and exited the car, I was surprised to see Mrs. Bee still where I had first noticed her.

Now, 'this should not be unexpected' I thought, the car still wasn't completely free of its layer of moisture, and I assumed that my little passenger was still stuck to the cars surface by moisture trapped under her. Again I was half persuaded to apply a little support with my forefinger, but decided against it as the old Monty Python mantra came in to my head that "Half a bee - philosophically, must *ipso facto* half not be!

It was the last part I wanted to avoid!

After I had obtained profuse thanks from the charity shop for the nice 'new' speakers I gave them (guilty - they looked good, sounded terrible!), I was on my way to the Bank.

My furry friend, stuck to the car, was still there when I parked and headed for the bank mangers office. Indeed, furry friend was still there when I returned!

I stood staring down at the quiescent creature wondering first how it managed to cling on to the car, and secondly - what possessed it to remain - if, that is, it could fly away?

I gave up grappling with the quandary and decided to get on with my periodic sojourn. With a can of paint in hand from the hardware store, I returned to the car to find that my furry girlfriend was still fixed to the metalwork. Another two miles of driving, this time in heavy traffic, and I was into the supermarket's car park.

I was a little preoccupied with what I had to buy - mostly with things that weren't on the shopping list I'd made before setting out (even so, I have never managed not to miss out an item on the shopping list!). So, as it was, it was only when I had trekked the requisite two miles around the store, packed the shopping away in the car boot and was looking forward to a coffee, that my eyes saw a little black speck affixed to the trim above the driver's door.

I found it hard to believe, but my little companion was still happily glued to the car, and appeared to have no intention of leaving.

As I looked closely at my friend, still apparently fully functional, I became somewhat worried that at this late stage of our journey something could happen to her. It was very unusual for a worker bee to remain static for any length of time unless exhausted by nectar harvesting, flight distance or heat exhaustion. I was suddenly taken by a sense of responsibility - after all, it was me that had kidnapped her and taken here away from her home. Now I was obligated to take her back, but very reluctant to risk her being shaken off on the journey home.

Should I try to capture her - put he in a jar and release her at the right time? Could I afford an attempt to pick her up? I had decided against that recourse earlier, and the reasons for not doing it remained unchanged.

Okay, it was her risk, if she had decided to stick it out on the window trim, who was I to interfere?

However, one thing was for sure, the car wash was off my schedule - the car was going to have to remain very dirty.

I kept my road speed well down on the way back, trying to reduce the air-stream over my tenacious stowaway - gambling that she would still be there when I returned home.

I pulled into our drive some thirty minutes after leaving the supermarket and carefully exited the car. As I looked down onto the window trim to my delight my faithful bee was still there.

I was so excited that I wanted my wife to hear the story before my star witness decided to depart. But just as I was about to call out, my wife suddenly appeared at the front door looking very excited.

"Come quick," she said breathlessly, "there's a huge swarm of bees collected around the trunk of the big apple tree and they've been there for hours...well, at least since just after you left."

The instant I looked at my wife I caught a black and brown speck rise up in front of me and fly off. As I attempted to track its flight path my wife began to wave her arm at me in exasperation.

What could I do?

My story was history - unsubstantiated it became a tall tale and no longer of any value. Resigned to consigning the whole saga to an after dinner 'You won't believe this but -.' I followed my wife into the house and through into the garden.

Sure enough, the apple tree was black with a massive, writhing swarm of bees, the whole assembly in constant motion like soft waves on nighttime seawater.

My wife had just commented on the unusual way the swarm was sticking to the one spot when I saw a small black dot diving down from above us. It landed on the swarm and blended in so quickly that it disappeared.

We stood and watched, as from that moment the swarm increased its movement, becoming increasingly agitated and active. Then, as if on some silent cue, there was a vast sound of countless bees lifting from the tree, and a black buzzing sheet soared upwards and away.

If you were to ask me whether I thought that the swarm were waiting for my passenger I will tell you that I am convinced that it was so. You would be justified in the rejoinder that the swarm could not possible know that one of their workers was on a car journey around the county and would be returning eventually. More to the point, you might say, how was it that my little friend was aware of the fact that eventually the car would be returning to home territory, and that the hive would be waiting for her.

I concede the argument.

My wife laughed when I told her of my experience and I suspect everyone else will. No way would a bee have the ability to predict future events, or to know that her kith and kin were anxious for her return.

Sure, officially, it was just sticky dew and old-fashioned coincidence that made the incident what it was.

However, if you ask me (and let's face it, I was the eyewitness) you will get a different perspective - it's my story and I'm sticking to it!

Accidentally On Purpose

My driving isn't the best, the number of narrow escapes I've had just driving along and minding my own business testifies to that.

Okay, the other drivers are equally at fault for having the impudence to occupy the space I wanted, but why they would want to collide with me when all I'm doing is utterly ignoring them is beyond me! I recall that a German expatriot working in Saudi Arabia left his car parked outside a shop - moments later it was promptly concertinaed by a large white Oldsmobile driven by a native. The German was convicted of 'reckless parking' by a Saudi court, being told, in their immaculate logic, that 'if he hadn't been in the country the collision would not have taken place'!

Of the major incidents in which I (reluctantly) plead guilty, only three were really bad. The first was when I was nineteen and late for a date with my girlfriend. I was in second gear and I stupidly used the accelerator as a whipping boy over my late departure from home (and inevitable complaints about my lateness by my girl).

As I stamped the throttle hard to the floor, the car took off with so much acceleration that I was pinned into the driving seat by the G force, making it impossible for me to react. Too late to brake, I shot into a roundabout (inner lane) and flew directly across two mercifully empty lanes, but perfectly positioned to mount the central circular reservation. I careened on, ploughing a twin furrow through all the flowers and shrubs.

The fortunately minor damage to my car was no consolation in any way. I received a massive bill from the council's parks and highways division (for fouling up their prize floral display) and an even bigger one from all the agencies involved in controlling incoming road traffic to the roundabout while a huge (and very expensive) crane retrieved my car.

If that wasn't a day to remember another certainly was. I completely wrote off a car driving to a Sunday shooting competition.

In those days, I was an avid rifleman, the proud owner of two competition rifles and membership of three rifle clubs that allowed me to shoot at more than seven different rifle ranges over the southern counties. On the day in question, I was on my way to the ranges finding myself driving over spectacular countryside with my rifles in the back of the car and six hundred rounds of loose 7.62 mm ammunition in an old box - balanced precariously in the passenger foot well. It was as I brought the car round a tight bend that the ammunition box overturned and hundreds of cartridges started to slosh around in the foot well, each one reacting to the car's movement.

I don't have to tell you that layers of loose cartridges, all on the move, constitute a deadly risk - if one lines up with the other, and strikes it hard enough from behind, there is the risk of not just one deadly detonation but hundreds, as one detonation initiates others.

It was as I was leaning over to the left, driving with one hand and trying to scoop up the cartridges with the other, that I came up behind a stationary car - and he was damn well occupying all of the narrow road width available! Of course, I braked hard - all the time imagining cartridges banging in to one another as I did so. But the only bang that occurred was as my car impacted the back of the stationary one. Fortunately, both our cars were just dented, and not so badly that they were un-drivable.

I made no attempt to explain myself to the other driver who disclosed, amid a stream of obscenities, that he had stopped to empty a painfully distended bladder. Nor did I blame him vocally (he was much bigger than me) for being a devils agent, nor for not being somewhere else (like three hundred miles away down a deep latrine). Instead, we dutifully exchanged details and he drove away, still exercising his full vocabulary of profanities.

Your right, I should have stopped to replace the cartridges in their box - but let the first of you without a similar sin throw the first stone!

So, I hear you say, what misdeed was associated with your third (reluctantly guilty) 'accident'. Well, none actually, and this is where my tale becomes a 'take it or leave it' because it's a true story, and even I couldn't make this one up.

I was on my way to the local University driving, if I remember correctly, a mustard yellow Fiat 124 Sports Spider, my pride and joy at the time (a clue to the period in question of course!).

Approaching a roundabout (my nemesis!), I carefully slipped in to the middle of the three lanes of a roundabout and steered towards the feed lane for my exit. As I did so, I caught the flash of a grey car body appearing on my right side. Without ceremony, or a 'by your leave' he then proceeded to side swipe me - twice! The noise was horrendous and I felt the car kick sideways as the impact forced me to the left.

The driver of the grey car hit his horn and also veered to his left forcing himself in front of me as I braked to avoid another, this time front to tail, collision. I came to a halt directly behind him.

We crawled through veering and hooting traffic to park on the outer lane of the roundabout between the second and third exit lanes. As I stopped, the other driver shot out of his car and came running towards me, forcing traffic to steer around him. I locked my doors using the manual 'all door' switch and wound down my window a little.

His was probably in his late twenties; his skin tone was sallow and his hair a lustrous jet black.

"What the fuck do you think you are doing... eh?" he spat out through my window gap in a heavily accented English.

"I might ask you the same question," I replied, "as I recall you hit me - not the other way round. Furthermore, if you insist on swearing at me and laying siege to my door I have no intention of discussing this with you."

"You little fuck, "he replied, "I'm going to - look what you did to my car!"

As he began to pull at my door handle, he suddenly looked to his left. Checking my rear view mirror, I saw a white police car draw up and a very heavyset policeman step out and adjust his cap and tunic.

I had simply glanced in my mirror for a few seconds but in that time my irate adversary had vanished. Long before the policeman had had a chance to walk up to my car, the one in front had screamed away in a cloud of dense, oil filled, smoke and disappeared through the roundabout's third exit.

At first I was disconcerted that the police car hadn't roared away giving chase. Instead, the policemen watched the departing car disappear and then tapped on my window.
I wound down my window (as above, this was before the days of ubiquitous electric windows) and looked up at the uniform above me.

"Just step out of the car for a minute sir - if you will." he said, calmly and politely.

"No problem at all." I mumbled, and unlocked the door prior to exiting. The door creaked badly as I forced the distorted panels and hinges to move and even so, it took some effort to push the door back far enough for me to vacate the car completely.

For the first time I saw the damage to the car and it almost made me weep. The whole of the body area, up to and including the drivers door, was dented and gouged. I stood looking at it in total disbelief and was only half aware of the policemen talking to me.

"Sorry - what?"

"I was saying sir that I need to see your license, test certificate and insurance documents."

"Sorry," I said, as what he was asking of me began to register, "I don't carry them with me."

"Right, name please."

I was starting to allow the distress of the incident (and my resentment) to build up some anger.

Why not?

First I get sideswiped, the other driver is not only entirely to blame but bloody abusive. Then a policeman turns up and behaves as if I am the instigator of the whole thing. Not only that, the perpetrator runs off and the cop does nothing about it!

"Excuse me sir," I managed to articulate calmly, "that car, the one that's just torn off down the exit there - it's possible you saw it - he sideswiped me just before you showed up and now you are treating me as though I'm to blame. Why do you need to waste time getting my details? What you should be doing is giving chase to the car that's just escaped. Are you blind officer, why am I at fault when you know full well it takes two to tango - look at my car, how do you think it got like this? "

He smiled - for the first time in my life I had seen a policeman smile. Strange this was, when in effect he was being told he was a complete moron.

"Don't be upset sir, I know what happened and you are not going to be charged or arrested. Getting your details is just a formality. We'll need your details and a statement for a prosecution."

I was slightly placated but now somewhat curious.

"You say you know what happened - but you weren't here when that idiot collided with me. How could you know?"

Again, I was privileged with a wane smile from the uniformed giant.

"I would think that the man who just collided with you is in custody by now. An unmarked police car was waiting for him...just after exit three - hold on."

He turned and mumbled something into his 'walkie-talkie'. I heard static - and a distant, heavily distorted human voice, which to me was totally garbled and incomprehensible, then replied.

The policeman understood it, I didn't.

"Yes, we got him. His name is Erin, Mathew Erin. Last night he got a skin full at his local watering hole and was so inebriated that he drove his car into a tree. Now, Mr. Erin is a clever man, so he thinks how do I get my car fixed without having to pay for it myself. Insurance did you say? No sir, not only has Mr. Erin five convictions for driving without insurance, at the moment he's only got third party cover if any at all. What he needs is somebody else's insurance - someone else to have to claim against. That's where you come in sir - a likely victim is identified, he crashes into you and then argues that all the damage to his car is down to the collision and your negligence, the earlier damage being indistinguishable from what happened later."

I was dumfounded. "So what you are saying is that he hit me deliberately?"

"Oh yes, no doubt about it."

So how did you know about him - what he intended to do I mean."

"We didn't - we're still after him for last night's mayhem - after he hit the tree he went on to bounce off four parked cars on his way home, causing more damage to his car and ruining four others."

"That's terrible," I moaned, "if he has no insurance, I'll have to make a claim for my own damage - I can't see my insurers believing a word I say."

"It's okay sir, we'll give you a criminal case number so you can have your insurers confirm that your car damage was the result of criminal action and we'll give you a 'no fault' status. They'll pay your costs without affecting your no-claims. Oh, and you'll have to appear in court as witness - if, and when, we get a conviction, we will all feel a lot better. The man's a menace."

The magistrates court was large, over hot and airless, all speech suppressed by a kind of dull reverberation that left any ensuing silence hanging like an ill-omened blanket.

On that morning, as the nasty Mr. Erin's case was due to be heard, I recall being in court with two police witnesses, the arresting officers, myself as victim and a small clutch of lawyers and court officials.

The magistrates looked tired and bored and everything went forward at an interminably slow pace. I eventually went in to the witness box expecting a grilling from the defending lawyer but even he gave the impression of fighting a losing battle. The sallow skinned defendant never said more than "No." or "I didn't" in the witness box and the defence was so implausible it was a foregone conclusion he would be convicted - and so he was.

A twelve-month suspended prison sentence and a substantial fine was imposed on him, though it left no one in any doubt that regardless of the sentence, he'd been treated too leniently and was very lucky.

I left the court somewhat disappointed and stood standing in the vestibule entrance leading to all the other courts in session that day. I had seen the sheet rain through the open doors leading from 'my' courthouse and decided to wait until the rain had abated before leaving.

As I kicked my heels, the sallow faced defendant came walking through the vestibule talking avidly to his lawyer. I caught none of the conversation but as he passed by he recognised me.

"Fuck you." he mouthed as he walked by.

I tried to keep my dignity.

"I resent that - whatever you got you brought on yourself."

He stopped, his lawyer now behind him looking somewhat concerned.

"What I brought on myself is a win on the lottery." he sneered, "I could buy and sell you right now so you can fuck off."

I imagine the look of disbelief on my face, turning to amazement as his lawyers expression confirmed what had been said, was sheer joy to him. He chuckled all the way out of the courthouse with myself slowly trailing him in the desperate hope of having the last word. But no riposte seemed possible - at least, I couldn't think of one.

At the courthouse doors, I saw him part from his solicitor with a wave, and then, under an umbrella, make for the car park. As he was lost from sight I reflected on the injustices the world allows - of all the likely winners in life, here was one thoroughly undeserved. It tested any faith I had in a just God.

I stayed in the vestibule longer than necessary - dejected and depressed by my recent experiences and smoking the last of my cigarettes. I stared out at the ominous black clouds and the constant downpours that burst driving rain unmercifully onto the speckled grey steps leading up to the courthouse and splashed into the vestibule.

From my position, I could look across the steps to the access roads coming in to the courts and the car park exit lane. As I listlessly scanned the outside world a new black

Jaguar nosed down the exit lane, intending to filter in to the traffic stream on the main road. As it did so, a four door Ford slowed to allow it in and the Jag moved forward to enter the traffic. Immediately the Jaguar moved the Ford accelerated, pulled to the right, came abreast of the Jag' and slammed itself hard in to it.

The screech of tyres and the explosive report as the two car body shells ground into one another could be heard well into the courthouse. I watched - fascinated by the spectacle and particularly uplifted by the fact that I had recognised the driver of the Jaguar as it had passed - it was my sallow skinned friend!

It didn't take long for the police to descend on the scene of the accident - after all, the courthouse was crawling with them. Indeed, even at a distance, one particularly large officer was familiar to me. The same one who was in court with me today, and had appeared at my encounter with the *nouveau rich* sallow faced Jag owner a few months back.

I had no intention of vacating my grand stand view of the proceedings and my glee rose minute by minute as I saw the unwilling drivers of both crumpled vehicles handcuffed, inserted into police cruisers, and driven away. Not long after, two large tow trucks appeared to begin moving the wrecks away. As I watched the Jaguar being hauled up the tow truck ramp by a powered winch, I was able to discern a definite twist in the body - the front nearside wheel was well off the ground. Indeed, as the tow truck carried out a 180-degree turn it was obvious that the Jaguar was so mangled that it was a 'write off'. The Ford had faired little better.

Some thirty minutes later all that was left was a policeman with a broom sweeping the road to remove the last of the glass splinters and other smaller debris. One police car remained, and as the broom and the sweeping policeman disappeared into the police car it turned back into the court access road. Slowly and deliberately, it drove up to the official pick up point at the front of the courthouse steps. I watched the two officers in the car laughing as they approached.

It stopped to disgorge the large frame of my friendly policeman, the one who had given evidence at the hearing of a certain Mr. Erin. He, exited at a fast pace as the rain began to beat down again. As he draw near to where I was standing at the side of the vestibule entrance, he smiled.

"Poetic justice?" I said.

"More than you know." he replied "The Jag was brand new and the driver of the Ford was also a known 'crash and claim' con artist - we've nailed him now for reckless driving. Our Mr. Erin is the real joke - he had a taste of his own medicine didn't he? His claim that he was deliberately sideswiped doesn't hold water - at least we prefer not to think so. He'll be charged with reckless driving too, and driving without insurance. His suspended sentence will be invoked and as for other charges, they will throw the book at him. How do you feel about that?"

The glint in the policeman's eye was a remarkable sight. Nevertheless, I had one reservation.

"Yes, but he will be released eventually and he's got a lot of money. I still don't think it comes entirely under the banner of natural justice."

The policeman smiled a broader smile.

"You might if you knew he now has sufficient resource not to plead poverty in a civil case. You can sue him for everything he's got - I would."

As I contemplated this interesting piece of advice a grey suited man came up to us.

"Sergeant, sorry to intervene - can I have word when you're done?"

My policeman friend turned to the newcomer. "Of course - ah..."

He then turned to me.

"Let me introduce you to Mr. Michael Marriott. Michael is a civil law barrister, who takes some cases *pro bono*, I'm sure he can help you. Call on me if you want any er... evidence. I'll tell Michael the whole story"

I smiled at both of them - it was my day after all.

Against The Odds

I was always interested in numbers; even as a boy I consistently made it as the top maths and science student at school, and when I had finished my time at University, with a PhD in statistics and numerical analysis, a large insurance company recruited me as a junior actuary. It wasn't my first choice, but the salary was stupendous and I was newly married.

The job was fairly straightforward and, truth to tell, boring. I was given vast amounts of data referring to everything from staff mortality rates in psychiatric hospitals to the number of female drivers killed in motor accidents while adjusting their makeup in rear view mirrors.

It was used to determine what potential liability might be incurred by the company in insuring various categories of people. Sometimes the risk was too great to actually provide insurance - we had no interest for example in insuring the lives of stunt men or those convicted of drink driving. Of course, it was all calculated to ensure the company made a significant profit from the insurance policies it did offer. High risk meant high premiums, low risk meant affordable insurance - after all, the company's ultimate strategy was to reduce it's settlement of claims to zero.

We never underestimated the risk levels. Premiums were always worked out on a standard formula that included the level of error in the data, the inherent risk factor (a numerical value), the cost to the company of composing and administering the policy itself, a scaling factor for the long term profit margin, and a built in safety factor to guard against the unexpected. Steeped though we were in statistical analysis, and good though we were in applying our mathematical skills, we all new what Mark Twain and others had said - that there were 'lies, damned lies, and then there were statistics'!

The behavioural distribution of large sets of populations in various professional, social and economic sectors was surprisingly predictable. As such, we were tolerably good at determining the likely trend of claims within the insurance categories we offered. So much so, that we actuaries could even work out what chance we, as a profession, had of getting promotion, winning the lottery or being divorced.

It was this last aspect that began to concern me.

My wife Alvena had been my University sweetheart and we had married a week after I got my PhD. She had been recruited by a publisher directly after she graduated, and her salary helped me to keep going financially for the three years I was a post-graduate student. We really clicked, and for a long while we were very happy. Then I began to get concerned that we were drifting a bit. The drift began after we had found a house and settled down to a routine life. Alvena became engrossed in a vast range of different hobbies, social obligations, charitable activities, publishers parties and book launches. Her job, and her other interests, took so much of her time that we hardly saw each other. Add to that the fact that our sex life had reduced to reluctant fumbles, and I was beginning to worry.

I found it impossible to get her to see how destructive things were becoming. I tried more dinners and unplanned lunches - she was always booked. I sent flowers and other things - she was never 'there' to receive them! I spoke about starting a family - but, she said, she had her career to think about and it was something she would consider in a few years time. In short, she deflected, or ignored, everything I did to try and regenerate our marriage.

Now this situation was beginning to affect me at work. I was so distracted at times that I had to revise some of my statistical computations repeatedly - something I seldom needed to do.

Alvena was too precious and important to me to simply ignore the problem. The one thing I didn't want was to be one more digit on the current statistical count I had for divorces in the UK.

As I pondered my options one evening in my little study at home, Alvena popped her head round the door and asked if I was busy.

"Not if you want to talk." I said

She came and sat on the old couch I had installed as a visitors pew - though it hardly got used.

"I have a confession to make." she said.

This sent a chill down my spine. Was this the 'I'm in love with someone else and I'm leaving' speech - the emotional confrontation I had dreaded for so long, a confrontation that was to end with 'I want a divorce'.

She smiled and with no little hesitation said "Darling, I've been less than truthful with you. The publishing company I work for isn't what it seems. I can't tell you every detail but we are actually part of the secret intelligence services and I'm really working for the government. It's a long story but I was recruited just after you started your post grad' at Uni' and I've been involved ever since."

It took me a full minute to register what she had just said and I could feel my mouth forming strange contortions as I tried to come to terms with what I had just learned. The best I could do was to mumble "Bloody hell Alvena" as I finally made sense of what she was saying.

She smiled. "I know this is a shock, and under normal circumstances you would have been kept out of what I am doing, but of late we have been grappling with some major incidents which have taken all our resource. I know I have been neglecting you for some time and I'm sorry. It was that or resign my job, and as things stood I couldn't desert the ship. Do you remember the murder of the under secretary of defence in the news recently? Well, he wasn't the real target, the minister was. The defence official who died in that M3 accident some months back? He was murdered too. In fact we now have seven prominent politicians assassinated... yes assassinated... over the past fourteen months. Fortunately, the time lapse has been so long that the media hasn't twigged that all the killings may be related. As you can guess darling, we don't want them to put two and two together, and we don't want any more deaths!"

I sat at my desk staggered by what I had heard.
"But all these parties and book launches - all the literary stuff you showed me - all a front?"
"Not really, we keep the facade credible by actually publishing the odd title, or promoting a new author. It's a necessary deception. In fact some of our people have no idea what goes on behind the scenes - they genuinely believe we do nothing but publish."

I was still a bit stunned by Alvena's revelations and could only shake my head and state the obvious.
"Okay - but now that I know about it, I'm in possession of information you would ordinarily have kept from me - where do I come in to all this hush-hush stuff?"
My wife could always swing my mood - she only had to smile at me and I melted into a soggy, emotional

slave. Her smile now was one I had been waiting for - for a long time.

"Darling, the Defence Minister is currently under close armed protection because we are certain that he is a potential target. The problem is that its no longer safe for him to move about as he usually would do. In fact, he's a prisoner in his own home and ministry. He has international commitments but we are wary of allowing him to leave the country by air. Our greatest fear is that the aircraft might be bombed or taken over with the consequential casualties. Commercial flights pose the highest risk but as things stand so too military ones - we can't even be sure that a military aircraft might not be sabotaged or bombed."

It all seemed reasonable to me but where did I come in to all this?
"I hear you my love - but again, where do I fit in, I'm an insurance actuary - not a security expert."
Again, I got a warm smile from a woman I loved and so I decided not to press the reject button too hard.
"Where you fit in is simple." she said, "You're a statistician
and we need to know one simple thing - apart from definite intelligence regarding an assassination plot, is there a statistical basis for deciding that the Minister can get on a plane or not?"

Alvena looked at me as she finished, and sat pensively as I considered the implications of her query.
I had to confess, it was a very interesting question - but was it valid? It was a bit like asking if statistics could predict the outcome of a trip by sea during the Second World War. Winston Churchill had survived a good many ocean passages with the odds stacked against him but he had gone just the same.

Why?

Because he instinctively weighed the odds as still being in his favour. Likewise, his movement by air was damned dangerous - but there were ways of reducing the risks by ensuring the enemy thought he was going to be somewhere else. Again, Field Marshall Montgomery; the odds on him were slim but he made them statistically less dangerous, and contrived a strategic deception, by having a double pretend to be where he actually wasn't.

I finally came to the conclusion I instinctively knew I was going to make anyway. "Okay - I'm listening, I'll look at the data and see if there is any way of lessening the odds for the Minister. You will have to give me a week or so, and I have one condition. No one communicates the results of any analysis I do to the Minister but me. Right or wrong, I present my findings my way - with my provisos and my stipulations."

That night I got my Alvena back. Strange, but we felt closer than for a long time - she no longer had to live a life of deceit and I was now allied to her cause. I was so relieved I almost forgot why it had happened.

But after a week I was no closer to establishing the probability factors involved - yes, it was one thing to determine likely airborne bomb threats, entirely another to reduce them to a minimum. It was even more difficult to include a factor where the passenger was a definite target and was not going to be indiscriminate bombing that was likely to take place. If the assassins were following a definite human target it was the target that put the aircraft at risk, not the other way round. It was the target's vulnerability that was the thing, though that in itself hardly changed the underlying statistics for all the world's aircraft flying at the time. It was frustrating. I wrestled with the fundamental query 'is there a statistical basis for deciding that the

Minister can get on a plane or not?' as if it were a pure statistical problem. It was only when I realised that it wasn't, that I saw a way out.

I was lucky - I had recalled some of my chemistry, and some of what I wanted I found in the garden shed - a very old bag of weed-killer. I then went to my local tyre and exhaust depot and begged some battery acid. They reluctantly complied after I offered a the need to purge a container and, more significantly, a large payment.

I had it all ready by the time I was due to meet with Alvena, her colleagues and the Minister.

I met Alvena at her office; surrounded by what for all intents and purposes appeared to be a thriving publishing operation. I was then shown in to her boss' office and everything changed. His name, so he told me, was Wellbeloved. A misnomer? Definitely!

He was well dressed, well groomed and formally polite - but loved? One thing was for sure; he had a hard, curt and uncompromising manner. Alvena, raised an eyebrow when he wasn't looking which said 'you think I would, or could, have an affair with this guy'?

With brief introductions over, we left and made for the underground car park. The car journey was mercifully short and our footsteps were soon echoing in the corridors of the Ministry of Defence. We were shown into a large and well-furnished office, well lit by high widows with views over the Thames.

I had seen him before, but meeting the Minister face to face proved that TV appearances could often create a false impression. His handshake and eye contact was firm and sincere and I felt the whole company relax somewhat when he kissed Alvena on the cheek and addressed me as 'the reason his wife's car insurance was so high'. "After all," he said as we were invited to sit down, "she only had two drink driving convictions and was as blind as a bat."

Coffee came in shortly after and a little small talk ensued. It was then that our pleasant and gracious host became the Minister. He took to his chair behind his desk and looked at me.

"Well, Doctor, did we set you an impossible task - are you going to be able to help us make up our minds? Can statistics indicate whether I will get on a plane... or not, one that is likely to blow up... or not?"

I put down my coffee and opened my briefcase.

As I pulled out the package Wellbeloved suddenly stood up and his hand went into his inside jacket seeking a weapon.

"It's okay." I said, "Your right, it's an incendiary - a bomb, but safe - it's not armed yet."

I heard Alvena gasp and saw the Minister suddenly drain blood from his face. Yet, he had the composure to keep his voice steady.

"What are you doing - what's the meaning of this?"

I stood, leaving the deadly package on the coffee table by his desk."

"Minister, you ask if there is a statistical basis for deciding whether or not you can get on a plane. Well, there is, but only indirectly.

It goes like this. As things stand, unknown assassins are targeting you, and with that in mind I calculate there is a thousand to one chance that you will get on a plane with a bomb hidden within it.

Were you not a definite target and flying on a commercial flight, I calculate that the chances of there being a bomb on board are ten thousand to one.

However, and here is the paradox, the chances of there being two bombs on any one plane, regardless of all other factors, works out to be one hundred million to one against.

In short Minister, if you want to be virtually 100% safe from a bomb when you travel, take a bomb with you! In fact, you can have mine. Taking your own bomb means it is nearly certain there won't be another one besides your own!"

I could have swum in the depth of silence, which followed my announcement, but it sunk home. I got a letter a week later from the man himself, conveying his thanks and noting that it was a good job he had diplomatic status. Otherwise, he noted, a search of his baggage as he boarded his flight would inevitably have resulted in his being arrested - on charges of terrorism!

Knight In The Night

She slammed the car door behind her, and was instantly engulfed in another onset of torrential rain. She pressed the key fob remote door lock as she began running for the shelter of the hotel entrance, but her haste was futile as the skies opened up even more, and the driving rain turned into a hissing, lashing, torrent.

Ten yards from the hotel entrance a rain obscured figure emerged and stepped onto the tarmac drive leading to the hotel. Using the figure as a guide to her destination, she tried to accelerate her pace but only managed to stagger as the flooding rain sloshed around her ankles and made one foot clip another. She was going to fall, and there was nothing she could do to prevent it.

Within a few paces of the entrance, she began to topple. As she did so the oncoming figure leapt forward and diving forward rolled under her. She shot out her hands and arms defensively but to her amazement, something prostrate under her cushioned the impact. Only the hard contact of the tarmac on one of her knees reminded her of how bad the fall could have been.

Against the clamour of the rain, she heard a slight groan as her fearless saviour attempted to turn. Carefully climbing to her feet she bent and tried to assist her fallen hero, a hero who was still stretched out on the ground. His grey overcoat was saturated from the deep puddles of rain he had ploughed into as he threw himself to the ground. The pelting rain had done the rest and she was still pulling at the sodden material when a voice said "Strange way to meet Miss Hardin - it is Miss Susan Hardin isn't it, I'm not mistaken?"

She was no less surprised at the query as when he had leapt to her aid.

"Er, no I'm not - why did you....?"

The darkened figure on the ground started to move and she stood back to let him get to his feet.

He scrambled to his feet without any sign of discomfort and as he stood erect, he was at least ten inches taller than she was. There was a moment of embarrassed silence as each stood face to face. The uncomfortable moment lengthened as both underwent further soaking and eye-blinking discomfort. Like seals just out of the sea, each motionless body rippled with reflected light and dripping water as the rain continued to bombard them.

His face was in deep shadow and she was unable to get an idea of his features, but one never looks a gift saviour in the mouth so she began her speech of appreciation.

"You saved my life, I'm so grateful - are you okay, you're not injured?"

He said nothing and she was ignorant of the fact that he was disregarding a momentary agony in the toes of his right foot. Nor was she aware that though the pain was in no way diminishing, he was not about to display any weakness by admitting he was injured.

Instead, she just detected a grimace on the shadowy face and decided it was appropriate to offer a reward. She leaned forward to ensure he heard her above the splattering rain.

"Look, I'm late for a date but no matter - can I reward your kindness with a quick drink?"

He hesitated, "Why not - we can drip rainwater all over the Hotel's carpets - we might even dry off a touch and, anyway, my appointment's probably long gone. Yes, shall we go?"

She was escorted into the Hotel foyer by a tall wet man who made soggy squishing sounds as his moving feet pumped water up through his socks and over the walls of his shoes. He quickly removed his topcoat and folded it into the crook of his arm. Straightaway, water soaked through to the lowest part of the sodden material and immediately began to drain onto the foyer carpet. He remained impassive and seemed to ignore his condition, as too the fact that the rest of him was no less wet. She removed her raincoat as well but found that she too had little to be pleased about. The fall on the tarmac and the teeming downpour had resulted in a blouse with wet shoulders and skirt heavy and crumpled from being waterlogged from the hem up.

The hotel bar was directly off the foyer and as they passed the baroque double doors and stepped on to deep, sponge like vermilion carpeting, they found the plush seating area virtually deserted. The bar was white and exquisitely fronted with stucco relief's. Behind it stood a barman polishing a glass and trying not to appear to be too attentive as they came in. A more bedraggled pair he had yet to see, but it wasn't his job to judge his customers.

"Good evening madam and sir - I see the weather has not improved. How can I be of service?"

Her tall escort turned to her. "What would you like to drink?"

She raised a hand in objection "No - I owe you a drink - remember?"

As she looked up at his face, she tried desperately not to giggle as she noticed a small stream of water draining off his matted hair and forehead, on to his left cheek, and making its escape by dripping off his chin. That equalled in entertainment by a large water drop that hung precariously off the end of his nose and swung back and forth as he spoke.

It was clear she was unable to break contact with what she saw and he smiled in anticipation of an explanation.

"Yes, I know, I suppose I look a sight. Certainly no girl would find me attractive now."

She smiled sympathetically "Oh, I don't know - I imagine you could be quite presentable once dried out."

He flashed her a smile in return, which had the effect of diverting the water running down his face and causing the water droplet on his nose to break free.

"And what about you?" With his free arm he made a neutral gesture at her lower body.

She looked down, aghast to see that her short skirt was stuck to both her thighs. Worse, her tights were torn away at both knees and, over stretched by the scraping on the tarmac, had now sagged into plump folds around her lower legs.

She looked up, certain he was gloating, but changed her mind as she looked into his smiling eyes.

"Never mind." he said "We could both do with a little renovation. Weren't you supposed to have an appointment tonight - no show?"

"Like you." she said, "I was late - perhaps it was for the best, I don't know."

"Perhaps - kismet?" he smiled again.

She stayed silent for the moment apparently in meditation. Then with a slight shake of her head, she broke the spell.

"Drink?" she offered. "Before we both dissolve."

"Oh yes... your round I believe." he turned slightly to throw his still dripping overcoat onto a nearby chair by her equally wet raincoat.

"Something warming for me I think." she said, turning to the barman who had patiently listened to the exchange with a bemused expression on his face.

"Sweet Sherry - schooner please and..."

"He dropped his head slightly in appreciation, "Scotch for me - double."

The barman nodded and turning to the array of inverted bottles behind the bar, began his work.

Shifting so that he faced her, he kept close and she made no effort to move away from him, indeed she began to think he was not bad looking. He in turn began to think the same about her.

"So - you aren't Sue Hardin - I have to admit it, I'm in no way disappointed. If I had to contend with a disaster tonight you would have to be the best consolation I, or anyone, could have had."

The barman silently placed their respective drinks on bar coasters in front of them and then, sensing their mutual attraction, smiled inwardly and drifted off.

They picked up their glasses and sipped, each looking at the other.

"That sounds like a sincere compliment." she said with a short laugh.

Replacing her glass on the counter she continued, "If you want me to, I can be your Sue Hardin - that is, until you find the real one."

"He smiled again, his face now drier and slightly flushed with the warmth of their surroundings.

"Really - that's an offer I can't refuse, indeed no. Miss Hardin, may I introduce myself, my name is Blake, Martin Blake. Let's see if the hotel can find a way of drying us out a bit... and then, how about dinner?"

Outside of the Hotel the rain persisted, lashing down and bursting on the tarmac surface like clear, glittering, daffodil trumpets.

Two cars arrived simultaneously both trying to get as close to the Hotel entrance as possible. The first braked viciously as the brilliant blue white headlights from the second swung round and blinded the first driver as they reflected off his rear view mirror. Unsighted, and unable to stop in time, with the car's wipers overcome by the weight of rain, the second car ploughed into the rear of the first.

The noise of the collision was drowned out by the deluge of wind and rain, which now had thunder sharing the atrocious conditions. A flash of lightning lit up the two cars and their earlier occupants as each driver looked down in dismay at the mangled metal now disfiguring the once pristine condition of their respective vehicles.

"I can't see why you stopped so fast - there was no need." she said trying to control a small handbag sized umbrella in the driving wind.

"I stopped because your headlights blinded me and I was unable to judge where I was going. This bloody rain didn't help either - why were you so close?

He was of similar height to her and appeared to be mystified by his turn of bad luck.

"I wasn't close - not until you hit the brakes as you did."

He bit his lip, reluctant to get into an argument with a woman and in truth harbouring a slight sense of guilt. Dear God, he thought, I get all the luck - the promise of a wonderful date and then this bloody business adds to he fact that I'm already forty minutes late.

She gave the cars one last windswept eye watering look and said "Look, we can't leave the cars like this - the hotel will insist we move them away to allow other visitors to drive up. We will have to try for the car park."

He looked around, "Well, one or two others have left their cars on the side of the driveway - why can't we?"

She gave an exasperated snort, and with a perfunctory "You can if you wish, I'm moving mine." pulled at the drivers door of her car.

Without abating one inch, the gusts of wind and rain, occasionally reinforced by ever increasing thunder, made her run for the hotel entrance three times the usual ordeal of escaping heavy rain. As she broke onto the tarmac drive and gave up trying to stop the wind inverting her umbrella into a cone, she glanced across to see the dark shadow of the man's car now parked tightly against the edge of the access drive.

She started to run, an unfamiliar exercise which in the terrible conditions she was in blasted and flattened her drenched clothing, and made her awkward and off balance.

As she approached the hotel entrance, a figure waited by the arched awning, watching her slosh through the puddles and small lakes of rainwater. She made one last effort to increase her pace and as she did so, one ankle clipped another and she pitched forward. Throwing her hands forward to break her fall, she suddenly saw a dark mass shoot forward and dive under her. She came to a stop on top of a soft heap that appeared to be talking.

There was no doubt she was on top of a man. Looking down, and watching the rain pour from her bedraggled hair onto the body below, she saw the face of the driver who's car she had just driven into. He lay on his back with her laying directly on top of him, and apart from the fact that the rain continued to assail them both they were fairly comfortable.

"Sorry." he muttered, "I can't believe that happened... but I suppose it could have been worse."

She had no idea what to reply, had he done it accidentally, deliberately of was he trying a sympathy ruse? Whatever the case, she was in a better condition than she might have been - the fall could have been lethal.

She rolled away and carefully regained her feet. He then rolled over to his front and arching his back hauled himself up from an 'all fours' position.

"I was coming to help - saw you making a dash and wanted to ensure you made it safely. As you lost your footing, I tripped and lost mine. Amazing really...my God, you're drenched."

The external lights of the hotel reflected off her wet clothing and, closely observing her rescuer, she was minded to reply in equal terms.

"You too - you're absolutely saturated."

"So I am!" he exclaimed, appearing to notice for the first time that he had become a piece of water infested blotting paper.

"Look, may I suggest we get into the hotel, dry off a bit, have a drink and exchange our details for the insurance claims."

She blinked water from her eyes and was happy to agree. She turned with her escort and they immediately made for the hotel foyer.

The night duty desk concierge watched as two more dripping individuals left a deep trail of water over his lovely, immaculate carpet but could do nothing to prevent it. He prayed for a change of weather - as things stood there was going to be a distinct likelihood that his foyer would turn into a mud splattered river, fit only for fish and hippopotamus.

He fixated on the couple with resentment as they walked straight into the bar without acknowledgement. As they disappeared from the foyer, he picked up the phone to demand that housekeeping appear immediately to soak up the water. On a day like this he thought, his divine hotel should be closed.

The barman was unable to believe his eyes when the two walked into the bar and made their way to he counter. Had it not been for the size of the male newcomer, shorter than the previous unkempt and dishevelled individual, the pair now in front of him presented an almost identical scene.

The previous two were in the dining room - he wondered if these two were meant to accompany them.

"Good evening madam and sir - I see the weather has not improved. How can I be of service?"

He grinned inwardly - wondering if his new customers were going to follow the exact ritual of his two previous patrons.

"Let me get these." said the man, smiling at the barman and unbuttoning his topcoat.

"G and T?" she said as if in query.

"Okay, G and T, and a Bourbon for me." he said removing his topcoat and throwing it over the nearest chair.

"Right sir." the barman responded, and with a slight sense of disappointment turned to his racks of bottled spirits.

She was too wet to worry any more and simply tried to ignore the appalling state she was in. He was little better, and resigned himself to an uncomfortable ninety minutes before he could get home, shower and change.

"Are you coping." he asked, looking at what he realised was a very attractive woman, not withstanding her drenched state.

"I'll survive." she replied, offering a smile of appreciation.

"Oh... I'm Michael Apton by the way... and I'm really sorry about your car. Still, small mercies and all that."

She looked at what was in fact a very good looking man, a real man - the kind she always hoped she would meet one day."

"Oh... me, I'm Susan Hardin, here supposedly to meet an admirer."

She blushed slightly and looked away.

"Strange - me too, I had a blind date but the bloody weather insisted I arrive too late. Same for you?"

She nodded, "Yes, traffic...slow driving, appalling conditions, impossible to make it on time."

He looked at her with dread thoughts churning through his mind. What he said now could define the rest of his life. He took breath and tried for a softly modulated, appealing delivery.

"Well, in a way we did make it - here you are, and here I am. Call it kismet...yes?"

She looked back at his shining eyes and nodded in agreement. "Suppose so," she said "but maybe right place wrong people?"

He searched for a counter to her negative perspective.

"No - I don't agree, we would be stupid to ignore the fact that it could be - even might be - the right place and the right people… wouldn't you say?"

She turned as the barman silently placed their drinks in front of them and then melted away. She took her G&T and threw it back in one go. He dispensed his drink in the same way, and as he returned the glass to the counter, he looked to see her reaction. Now seeing she was struggling to find a reply, he had to press on.

"Have dinner with me now - that's if you don't mind staying damp for a while - pretend I'm your admirer. Please."

She had taken the idea of loyalty as far as it realistically could go. The truth was she had no allegiance to someone she hardly knew or liked and had failed to appear. The man now standing by her side was all that she would have wished for had he been her date. What had she to lose?

She turned and smiled. "Dinner? Yes, if you wish. But let's try and dry off a little before we eat, perhaps the hotel might help. Do you think they serve - oh, we'll see. Barman, concierge and dining room please."

The barman took the ten-pound note left in payment and waved his right hand. "Return as you came madam and thereafter it's the door to your left. As I recall there are only two others in there, they've still to finish I believe but should do soon."

Thanking the barman they made there way back towards the hotel entrance, noting that as they negotiated their way over the carpet, the path they were taking, and the one leading to the dinning room, was already marked by a pronounced trail of water.

Bedraggled and unkempt, and on view to all and sundry, they arranged help at the front desk utterly without embarrassment. Each cared less about their appearance as it dawned on them that on a filthy night, in impossible circumstances, fate had handed them the opportunity for lasting happiness. Only minutes passed before they had warm towels, some privacy and were looking forward to a hot meal.

As the concierge supervised the cleaning of the foyer carpet the hotel's maintenance supervisor appeared and walked up to the desk.

"Did Olson move that low concrete base for the parking barrier by the entrance. I told him to report to you when he had."

The concierge shook his head. "Haven't seen Olson at all, anyway he's sick isn't he, I'm sure I saw him listed as off duty for the next few days, and anyway he's house keeping, not maintenance. It's not his job."

The maintenance supervisor grunted in exasperation. "Look, we're short handed, it was a simple task and wouldn't have taken him more than a minute. Jesus, I suppose it's still there in the dark. Anyone could trip over it and do themselves an injury. That won't do us, our public liability insurance, or our reputation any good."

"You're damn right." the concierge replied "we'd better move it and quick, leaving it there won't do any damned good at all!"

Experiment

Those who have any knowledge of technological history, particularly the development of the telephone (as attributed to Alexander Graham Bell) will see the parallel in this short story. We recall that the first clearly intelligible words spoken through an experimental telephone were (so Bell claimed) to his assistant Watson - "Come here Watson - I need you." Though it was a profound invention that was to change our lives on Earth, elsewhere in the universe it could conceivably have an even greater influence.

It had taken all the resources, tenacity and patience the world had.

Seventeen generations had toiled, struggled and died in the endeavour. Many had despaired that it would ever become a reality, and many had asked if the sacrifice was worthwhile. But persevere they had and, against all the odds, the day they had anticipated through generation after hopeful generation, was drawing nearer.

It had been the great seer D-ven, the greatest of the clan thinkers who, seventeen generations earlier, had predicted that the warm mantle of liquid nitrogen that surrounded their world was the primary barrier to controlling electron transport and that as the temperature elevated many materials would become more and more resistant to electron flow. This one revelation had induced more brilliant minds to examine the effects of high temperatures. Then D-ewar, after a series of dazzlingly elegant experiments, had announced that having studied the properties of many non-metals at the intensely hot temperature of liquid water, he had determined that electron flow became negligible.

So that was it.

It was possible to inhibit electron transport.

But to take D-ven's predictions further it was necessary to evolve a mechanism that would confine the movement of electrons, and simultaneously inhibit the constant flow that occurred at normal temperatures. This took three generations and the combined effort of all the tech clan and their progeny. Then came the breakthrough.

A young upstart in the science clan, having only been adjudged competent to contribute to the problem of charge modulation for one planetary cycle, accidentally allowed the second atmospheric element, oxygen, to leak into the high temperature apparatus. As it did so, it broke the magnetic screening and created a powerful para-magnetic coupling between the solid mercury conductor and the planets magnetism. The resultant magnetic field, massive by any standards, deflected the electron flow. Thus was born the magnetic modulator - the penultimate requirement for the apparatus predicted by D-ven and his successors. On the day that it was discovered that the modulated electron stream could form its own time varying magnetic field, they knew they had all the elements needed.

Now, as the 17th generation progeny broke out from their shells under the weak, distant sun, the exalted first scientist spoke before the council of elders.

"We are close – very close to being able to overcome the difficulties of psi communication. If, what we are about to do succeeds, our enemies on the second planet will not be able to learn our dispositions fast enough to disrupt our strategy. It will mean we can use low-psi operators and deploy our forces in a way invisible and unintelligible to the second planet. They will find it impossible to counter our first strike."

As the words sunk in the council members felt a sudden elation – it appeared that all the time, sacrifice and deprivation was now justified. Each grudging permission by their 17 generations of forebears, to allow the work to continue - and each deaf ear turned away from the people's resentment and criticism - had now been vindicated. What they had hoped for was soon to be realised. If it meant the elimination of centuries of second planet domination, it was worth every black day it cost.

Slowly, and with infinite care the network of independent stations was constructed, each taking a team of psi atrophied beings. All were painstakingly selected, each unable to effectively communicate telepathically. At one stage the whole project faced disaster as it was realised that there might be insufficient energy projectors to energise each station. However, this was overcome when it was discovered that the new progeny had within it a small set of particularly powerful trans-radiators able to suck heat from the atmosphere.

Thermal insulation between stations also created problems, as too the problem of periodic field reversal in the planetary magnetism - it meant that the timing of the experiment would be crucial. Only when the field was at its maximum could the modulation be certain to work. As such, a time was set and everything depended on it.

As each station was finalised, and the various teething troubles were eliminated, it became apparent that there was neither the time, nor the opportunity to test everything. Too much depended on the second planet not being aware of the activity - or the intention - surrounding the apparatus. Ideally, a test run would have proved the system, but this tempted fate too much. Instead, each station was individually calibrated and measured against an exacting test standard that, because no two stations were coupled together, could not radiate information to the enemy. As the exercise was completed, the first planet waited in trepidation, listening and anticipating a ferocious response.

But nothing happened.

The second planet remained silent and inactive. It had been denied the lift in overall psi tension – the crucial signs of rebellion.

It was written in the glorious history of the first planet that the moment of victory came swiftly and inexorably. That the apparatus was constructed without delay and without protest and that the promise inherent in D-ven's prediction was a foregone conclusion.

But histories are often bland and convenient, and gloss over unpalatable truths.

In reality, the period following the exalted first scientist's promise to the council, and the completion of the system, had a devastating effect on the population. For to complete the system every spare scrap of resource the planet had was commandeered and poured in to commissioning the stations. It took every quantum of energy from everything that meant life and existence.

Already deprived, almost to the point of extinction, the beings of the first planet waited in stoic misery, as everything was made ready to retaliate against their hated planetary neighbours. Many never survived to see the day of victory, but for those who did it was a moment sweet in its simplicity.

Twenty-two full cycles after the council heard the exalted first scientist make his announcement, the day came.

It had been well thought out – no being with radiant psi was involved in the strategy. None in the tactical arm were given plans and it was expected that those that did deliberate on what disturbed the psi equilibrium merely provided a plausible deception.

During the time the second planet's psi sensitives were detecting the usual neutral emanations from the first planet, the first planet's secret group, attached to the exalted first scientist, were finalising their arrangements.

B-ell, the exalted first scientist knew he could not relay information that might compromise his people in the event that everything failed. If the second planet subsequently crushed the rebellion, the ruling families were expected to take the blame - but how to avoid a general massacre?

It was B-ell's assistant, the son of a distant forebear named W-at, who offered a gambit that would not, and could not, be perceived as the instigator of a general insurrection. A coded communication was the simple solution, a cipher that said 'strike', but to other out-world ears could be made to appear innocent.

At the mid cycle, with everything optimal, the experiment was prepared. Waiting for the moment, B-ell stood by the modulator and waited for confirmation; confirmation that all the preliminary tests were complete and that all that could be done had been done. As verification came, he took in a warm sac of oxy-nitrogen and exhaled it with clear intonation.

A thousand miles away, on the dark side of the planet where all the attack forces were gathered, his assistant heard his chief's modulation "W-at-son – come here, I want to see you!" And the war started.

Past Whispers

Clinging by loose and corroded screws to the pockmarked Victorian facade and its rusting platform canopy, mournful insect stained station lights fought a loosing battle against the oncoming early morning fog that shrouded the old terminus.

The platforms, now empty and devoid of bustle, bristled with scaffolding and suspended walkways; the legacy of construction crews who over the weeks had worked their way laboriously from one end of the station to the other. Now, as the night clung on, each poorly illuminated maze of tubing, hanging electric cable and temporary decking seemed to depict the frozen outlines of massive limbed insects and praying mantises; where seemingly every shadow black corner hid a monster.

Only the waiting room was so far untouched by the contractor's sledgehammers. Still sacrosanct, it waited and watched as the soot-blackened station received its first major renovation in over a hundred years.

Now, as the beginnings of a false dawn had slowly appeared, he ignored his numbed, stiff legs and walked towards the old waiting room. The enveloping pitch-black night had been cold, damp and clammy, now made worse with a bitterly cold winter breeze that crept through clothing onto flesh and bone.

He was not intent on finding a refuge as such, rather he had a job to do, and having to endure an hour wait before the first train on service pulled in to the station at six a.m., he could do both.

It was the inviting lights and the still glowing fire of the waiting room - which he espied through a smeared and grimy, paint peeling window frame - that offered the satisfaction of duty done followed by the respite of a comfortable wait.

He paused before the door, feeling a presence - as if an entity was confined to the old Victorian waiting room and somehow it was aware of his appearance. He hesitated before entering, feeling now the clamour of anticipation that leaked from the inside.

He closed the door on an empty room, seemingly bereft of any bond to time or space. He felt a tangible but gentle silence that descended on him and pervaded his whole being as he stepped in. It was a tranquillity that not only excluded the world outside, but gently echoed the whisper of innumerable souls who, over countless decades had experienced a myriad of emotions in their journey from one place to another. He sensed it all, the agony of lost love, fear of the future, the anticipation of new beginnings and the unyielding burden of misery and despair. Yet, behind all the mix of desperate emotions he felt resentment - the resentment of his being there to witness all the private remembrances.

As he waited, the voices of the past spoke to him, those now gone still able to pluck at his feelings and make him reluctant to intrude further.

The fire in the old Victorian grate suddenly flared up, and as it did so a single voice came to him.

"Begone," it said, "leave us to our memories or be one with us and reveal yours."

He hesitated, and then took the challenge.

Striding past the fire, the worn armchairs and the threaded rugs and carpet, he found the epicentre.

He stopped and closed his eyes, projecting the memories and experiences of a lifetime to those around him in the room. Soon his spiritual essence had joined the voices and he had taken his place among those now gone. He let them feast on fresh incidents, episodes, sorrows, sentiments and passions, and made his mark as yet another spirit; also to be heard if ever a different soul might came to listen. But then the voices started to become forlorn and despondent as they greedily exposed his reason for being in their presence.

He suddenly felt a weight of threat and it gave impetus to his legs. He rapidly exited the room, returning to the windswept and unwelcome station platform. He strode on, still partially enveloped in the ever-diminishing remnants of those he had betrayed. Eventually he came to a bench seat protected by a wall; away from the worst of the chilling and spiritually numbing breeze.

He had never before experienced so great a clamour of spite and resentment. He'd felt loss before, but this time he had been drowned by a tide of emotion; it had forced him to vacate the warmth of the old waiting room. The growing din of outrage had swamped his soul and his being. At the end the voices had screamed at him for bringing his treachery, for showing them that their collective accumulated memory was doomed to annihilation in a few days.

It was inevitable - he knew it, and what he knew could never be concealed from the voices.

A paranormal sensitive he might be, a keeper of memories; but even sensitives had to make a living, and demolition was his trade.

He always ensured he had the feel of a building before he demolished it - just so he could remember its soul.

After all, someone had to do it.

Take It To The Limit

Every day I collected the detritus of four children and two adults. My old washing machine swallows soiled school wear, playwear, underwear, work clothing, sports gear, bedding, soluble washing capsules, fabric softener (and magically, never to be found again, the odd sock!).

I had no need to programme the ancient machine, no need even to think about the grinding routine of wash day. It had become (and was) entirely automatic - load the drum, snap the door shut, confirm no one had tampered with programme six and push the 'power on' button.

As always the machine made a peculiar 'clunk' as the wash programme began and the first stream of water descended through the inlet valve and through the labyrinth of waterways into the drum casing. As the water began to fill the drum, the first tumble action would start and water would invade all the smelly fabric. This resulted in the day's first reminder that this was only the beginning of an ordeal, for a pungent, malodorous smell, would constantly leak from the machine. It heralded the end of 'dirty', and the beginning of 'clean' - which meant in turn (may God help me) piles and piles of ironing.

This then was my cue, for it was this daily event that signalled the shackles of the morning drudge - the ritual that was likely to be with me tomorrow, the next day and eternal days after that.

My rationale had told me not to be so pessimistic, after all, the family had to grow up some time didn't they? But then, the arithmetic told a different story. Six kids, possibly up to the age of eighteen, plus two adults for probably 300 days of the year meant a total number of washes (and the resultant piles of ironing) nearing 5000.

It was daunting, intimidating, overwhelming and utterly disheartening. I had visions of me at the age of fifty odd, wrinkled and worn out and still listening to that damned machine going 'clunk' as it started up. Nevertheless, my solace was the certainty that the machine could not endure forever, and in that event the ritual would be broken albeit temporarily.

It was a Friday, I remember, that matters came to a head. As usual the laundry baskets were nigh on overflowing and I piled all the laundry in front of the machine ready to separate the coloureds from the whites and the towels from the underwear. As the first pile was sorted - after estimating the weight, I was pretty accurate after years of experience - I threw in the first mouthful of clothing that the machine was going to chew up and digest. Wash capsule and fabric conditioner followed, and purely on autopilot, I slammed the door shut, waited for the red indicator to show it had interlocked, and hit the power button.

Nothing happened.

Now this was unexpected. The years of repetition doing this chore meant that I was one huge conditioned reflex - a fresh cup of tea was my diversion - and I had half made for the teapot when I realised that the 'clunk' had failed to occur.

I turned back to the machine and saw that the power on indicator was definitely illuminated. Likewise, the programme indicator was set to 'six', the door interlock display was showing, and as far as I could see, all was as it should have been.

I decided to start again and repeated the 'start machine' ritual but to no avail, It simply stared at me and refused to start. This was exasperating if not deeply frustrating. Mountains of unwashed stuff I did not want - I had a terrifying vision of months of soiled clothing growing into a vast mound of stinking, decaying textiles, occupying every room in the house and defeating gallons of deodorants.

No...I say again, no! It was too much.

I gave the machine a good kick while it was powered up and to my relief heard a distinct 'clunk'. However, this was a false dawn, because it was followed by a short period of silence that, in turn, was suddenly interrupted by the start of a spin cycle.

As the motor whined and kicked the tumbler drum into life it started to rotate. I stood transfixed by the event of a lifetime - the machine had finally gone wrong! The wash cycle was dead - long live the spin cycle!

But, this was not necessarily good! My dream of a respite from the daily grind centred on a brand new washer/drier, able to alleviate the need to dry everything in the garden, or the bathroom, depending on the weather.

Where was the flaw in my dream?

My husband of course!

Money, as always, was at a premium and nothing was bought unless it had to be - particularly electrical items - for he would even moan about the increased electricity bills! So, things as they were, I had to contrive a 'had to be' situation. It might require a little sacrifice here and there - but so what?

I was quick to realise that for me to have the chance of a less arduous life I needed a dead machine; more accurately, an un-repairable machine. In short, a defunct antiquated model with the consequential imperative of being replaced by a wonderful new washer/dryer; able to process and spill out dry, sterile, unwrinkled clothes that smelled of freshness and hygiene.

As I thought on this, the tumbler in the machine had started to rotate relentlessly and, as usual, the whole machine was vibrating violently with the spin. But as I watched, the spin started to increase to ever-greater speeds, and with it the whole machine started to walk away from its location between the two kitchen work surfaces.

As I backed away from the creeping white monster, the spin reached the peak with an eardrum-rupturing whine and the whole kitchen became blanketed in a cacophony of machine made reverberation.

I was tempted to try and outflank the machine and pull out the plug to disconnect the power, but I could see that the longer the present condition prevailed, the better chance I had of a complete machine 'write off'.

I decided to wait and see whether leaving things alone might work in my favour, so I stood and watched as the machine wobbled forwards. My ears continued to be assaulted by a cacophony of noise that would have shamed a rock band with ten thousand watt amplifiers.

The rotation of the tumble drum seemed to increase even more and so too the forward movement of the whole machine. I could see that the power lead was starting to straighten out and stretch away from the wall socket. Then, just as the plug was about to pull free, the machine gave a sudden lurch, accompanied by a tremendous internal explosion of disintegrating components. Large dents, flaking rust and artic white paint suddenly appeared on the top and sides of the casing as the internal mechanics fragmented and struck the covers. Then, as the motor and tumbler drum broke lose from their brackets and bearings, all electrical connection was ripped away and the machine expired.

I stood riveted to the spot by the terrifying episode, viewing a now lifeless appliance that was parked in the middle of the kitchen floor with all the appearance of having been through a fifteen round bout with a scrap yard bulldozer.

It was a miracle - here was my deliverance, my dream come true. No one could deny that what stood in the middle of the kitchen floor had not been contrived. My hubby would have to accept that I had undergone a terrible experience having been chased around the kitchen by a manic washing machine (I lay it on thick!). And then would come his rejoinder, the half hearted post mortem; attempts to allocate blame, all followed by resentful grumbling and a grudging acceptance that money would have to be spent to replace the old machine. Implicit in this was would be my insistence that it had to be a new washer/drier, and it had to be installed quickly or no one in the household got clean clothes.

We took the kids and ourselves to the local electrical superstore the next day and spent a happy ninety minutes looking at all the models, and frequently extracting our youngest from the inside of a tumble drier.

One of the sales assistants was very knowledgeable about the store's products and as we discussed things he enquired about the make of washing machine we had used previously.

On being told what make and model we used he smiled sympathetically.

"Oh dear, my mother used one of those - do you know, the damned thing actually chased her across the kitchen, blew up and injured her leg. As I remember, there was a class action court case about it, the company had to set aside a fund to compensate all those who had suffered injury or trauma because of that model's poor design. Yes, my mother received quite a payout from the manufacturers."

My husband and I looked at one another as if suddenly enlightened, and within minutes had been given the manufacturers details and claims department by our friendly sales assistant.

It was a fair exchange. The salesman got commission from the sale of a nice new tumble/drier while we waited three months during which our claim was processed. The loss adjusters inspected the old machine and reported that it was indeed an indisputable design fault causing a subsequent dangerous breakdown. I claimed traumatic stress (a few tears when the inspector was looking) and this was never disputed.

When we received the cheque, amounting to a very considerable sum, I concluded that my desire to see the end of that old machine was ideally timed. It appeared that there was a limit to the claims period and we almost missed it. Another week and we would have been unable to make a claim.

The cheque was made out to me and I made sure I banked it. Though my hubby grumbled more than usual, he was placated when I shared the award with him and he was able to buy a decent second-hand car for a change and still have lots of 'rainy day' money left. Of course, the kids had their bit and everyone was happy.

I always wondered if the machine knew about the cut off date for claims, or was it simply tired of knowing how much I hated it.

Whatever the case, my dream came true - we were so well compensated that I now send all our washing to the local laundry and I enjoy my mornings virtually free. However, sometimes I might be seen in the kitchen polishing a rarely used and pristine washer/drier - I do it simply to remind myself of how things might have been!

Sixteen Tons, And What Do You Get?

Old Nigel Allison was retiring - so they said! But it was hard to believe. He was a fixture in the paint works having been here all his life, and everyone thought he was likely to die in harness.

He'd done every job in the place at one time or another, and was in effect a walking encyclopaedia, not only of works operations but the repository of works history and lore. It was this which made him so valuable, and why it was expected he would be kept on by management way past his official retirement age. It was well known that at one time he'd saved the company piles of money by recalling the exact sequence of polymer binder deliveries from the suppliers, noting that it was one too many. Ordering the excess delivery away meant that the mixing vats didn't overfill with binder, thereby ruining a very large and expensive batch of brilliant white paint.

And yet, we had it confirmed in a works canteen notice that Nigel was definitely due to go. His retirement ceremony was arranged for the coming Friday and everyone was invited to attend. We all thought it was the passing of an era -that without Nigel the place simply wouldn't seem the same.

We used to watch him tirelessly operating the inlet valves for the paint pigments in a constant and perfectly timed sequence. There were five valves in all, each a manual valve operated via a relatively long handle that protruded through a Perspex safety screen. He never seemed to get bored or fail in his concentration - as the feed indicator lit he reacted smoothly, getting the sequence spot on every time.

When the retirement ceremony came round, and we all stood in the canteen listening to the Managing Director read what was a very humorous and complimentary speech, no doubt many of us wondered if we would get the same treatment when we left. After all, Nigel was the last of the old guard and we sensed that change was afoot. Eventually, we were going to have to modernise or let the competition walk all over us. Everything we used was antiquated. We were still using the same techniques and equipment that Nigel had seen when he started as an apprentice.

We knew it was coming and, not un-expectantly, it came a week after Nigel Allison had left.

The first newcomer I encountered was one of three unfamiliar faces that turned up on a Monday morning armed with a wad of plans and a clipboard. Dressed in blue coveralls, they moved systematically through the factory looking at each of the five process areas. They examined everything, making copious notes about each structure and manufacturing stage. Flow diagrams and area volumes were determined and, at times, it was like watching ants swarm around every silo, pipe, valve, chute and conveyer. They even sized up the mixing vats by crawling in as they were emptied and purged.

Then one day I came in to see a 'Mr. Blue coverall' looking at the inlet valves behind the Perspex safety screen. First, he looked at the valves, and then at his clipboard drawings then again at the valves and back to his clipboard.

He saw me watching and came over. He was tall, mid forties and had a pleasant smile.

"Hello, tell me, those five handles over there, they operate the pigment inlet valves yes?"

I nodded.

He smiled. "Who presently takes charge of them?" he asked.

"At the moment our shift - only those with previous experience - but that goes for most of the shift. We didn't always do it; it was the job of a guy who has just retired. He was on it for almost forty years."

The man smiled again - and wrote something on his clipboard. It was obviously something he found amusing because the wide smile never left his face.

"Forty years you say?" he queried.

"As close as we can say - he only retired a week ago and he was the last of the original workforce."

"Okay then... you have been very helpful, I'm grateful." Again, I was granted another, broader smile and he walked away.

This encounter was soon forgotten but a few days later I was summoned to the production VP's office.

As I knocked and entered I was greeted by the VP and two others, one of whom I knew - having met him earlier that week by the pigment inlet station.

"Ah - Michael." The VP always used out first names - he thought it made us feel important.

"Please -take a seat, we want to pick your brains."

I was a little unsure of that so I kept silent.

"Let me introduce Mr. Wyatt and Mr. Enfield - they are from our consultants evaluating our production, and planning what we need to do to er...improve matters."

All I could say was "Oh yes?"

"Yes - I'll let Mr Wyatt continue."

The man who had smiled so much in front of me earlier in the week was now more serious. He did give me a slight smile, but it was fleeting.

"May I call you Michael? You see Michael, we have noticed something rather peculiar. Do you remember who taught you the pigment inlet sequence when you first started it? Come to that, who taught the rest of your shift to do it. Was it our man Nigel Allison?"

It was, and I said so.

"Right." he said, "But I'll bet a large amount of money no one knows who taught him."

"Doubt it." I said, "Nigel started here forty odd years ago as an apprentice, God alone knows how he gained all his experience. What's this about - did Nigel do wrong somewhere?"

They all smiled in unison.

"No - not wrong but we have found out that whatever he thought he was doing he wasn't, and whatever effect he thought he was having was not quite what he thought it was."

After that mysterious revelation they told me the whole story and persuaded me to do it.

I didn't want to and they agreed that it wasn't imperative, but pointed out that it was better he be told officially rather than finding out by the back door.

And so I found myself knocking on Nigel's door one Saturday morning.

Unfortunately for me, he answered the door, gave a snort of delight, and invited me in.

He offered me a chair and a coffee in his living room and soon we were talking about old times. I dreaded the moment but, inevitably, it came.

"So, to what do I owe the pleasure then Michael - anything up?"

I decided not to be circumspect - better to dive in.

"Nigel, we have had consultants in the paint works assessing everything for modernisation. They came across the pigment inlet station and analysed it. They want me to tell you that...."

Nigel smiled - leaning forward to encourage me to finish. "Come on boy - I won't bite."

I hesitated and then carried on.

"They found...that of all the five inlet valves only one was actually functional, the rest had no connection, or had been disconnected decades ago. In short, you were carrying out a task that was virtually futile, and you did it for forty or more years."

There wasn't a flicker of a response on his face. Instead, he fell back in his chair and fixed his eyes on me.

"Don't be damned silly." he said, "I knew that, I disconnected them forty years ago when the pigment mixing was automated. Christ, it was the easiest job in the plant - wouldn't I have looked stupid teaching people to pull just one handle when a light came on - and how long would I have had a nice cushy number, with job security I might add, if anyone had realised that it was so simple. The guy I was originally apprenticed to only taught me one cardinal rule - 'make yourself indispensable'. God, that man spent fifty years lubricating shaft bearings that never turned and replacing electric motors that had no use at all. In fact he maintained half a plant that did nothing!"

I was agog, I laughed - I couldn't help it.

Nigel had sown up his job spec forty years ago by letting everyone believe he had his finger on every operation in the plant. But in reality he wasn't actually doing much. It was ironic, and I laughed some more when I realised that all my shift, and a good few others in the plant, had been taught by him to do exactly nothing in particular! Then I stopped laughing when I realised that it was going to take some clever work to ensure the same strategy in the new plant. But then, Nigel was still here and all we had to do was pick his brains.

Break Time

"For heaven's, sake will someone get me a coffee."

It was Stephen Jenkins, our boss, once more pulling his hair out over the firm's finances.

We were a small outfit, just seven strong, with an outstanding expertise in industrial process design. Martin, John and myself had PhD's and except for Cathy and Susan our administrator and factotum respectfully, only young Martin Fells was undesignated - he had a good degree in engineering and served as everyone's menial.

Stephen, the firm's founder was very experienced and spent most of his time vetting our work, while my two colleagues and I spent most of our time working out what it was he actually wanted us to do!

Miracles mostly, and sometimes even we had to acknowledge that the impossible we could do, but miracles took a little longer than Stephen liked.

It was on a Friday morning that Stephen called us all together for what we thought was a pep talk. Instead, he opened his address with the subject of our working practices, in particular our 'drinking' and office management.

Now when I say 'drinking' I don't mean we were all on the verge of becoming alcoholics.

It was worse than that.

We were all inveterate and incurable coffee drinkers, and we all consumed massive quantities every day.

To feed this huge craving of ours we had a long vinyl covered table set aside in the office kitchen, butting up to the other side of one of the office walls. This table was usually loaded with three coffee percolators, all constantly

90

bubbling away and being frequently replenished from an electric coffee grinder.

It came black - very black. Everyone liked it that way and we drank it by the gallon.

The only problem was that no one seemed to care about the recurring coffee dribbles that marked every surface in the office, nor the fact that the kitchen and office floors were stained brown from slops, coffee grounds and the dust from the grinder. In fact, the floor was so rough from coffee grounds that a tap dancer would have loved it.

So here we were, Stephen telling us in a very reasonable way that he wanted a major purge of our office. He wanted it cleaned up (clients were being put off by the poor hygiene) and, to make it easier to keep the office spick and span , he was going to install a coffee vending machine!

God! That almost scared the hell out of us.

A vending machine! We were going to have to pay for our coffee?

"Don't worry," he said, "there will be no charge to anyone, and think about it - no cleaning of cups and mugs (we didn't anyway), no mess in the kitchen - in fact, a better, more convenient and economically effective solution."

He was very pleased with himself and though we had the odd doubt, no one complained or objected to the proposal.

It turned up about a week later.

Two men, a trolley, and lots of boxes delivered themselves through our door and with slow abandon (they stopped every three yards to discuss progress) steered a pristine, chromium clad, vending machine into the kitchen. Thirty-five minutes later they had Stephen signing the acceptance forms.

They told Stephen that the machine would be cleaned and replenished automatically every seven days by an operative. Then they cheerfully said their goodbyes to everyone and disappeared without any instructions on how to operate the gleaming newcomer or what to do in an emergency. We presumed that they took the use of a vending machine on the same level as learning to write - everybody had to do it, and could do it. It was part of everyone's basic education!

True enough - and no one seemed to have any difficulty in extracting a cup of black coffee, or eventually throwing the empty polystyrene cups into the nice big waste bag hanging by the vending machine.

The next day I turned up for work at my usual time of ten minutes late and detected a sullen silence in the office. Susan was sitting behind her desk with a plastic mug held delicately in a two-fingered grip. As I walked in she looked at me as if to impart some important news.

"What's the matter?" I whispered, keeping in with the sense of dread that pervaded the office.

"Martin had a terrible argument with Stephen last night just after you left. I was just going home myself when it erupted.

I thought they were going to fight but it just subsided into a brooding disengagement. It's no better this morning, Stephen has locked himself into his office. Martin is in too but he won't talk about it."

This was not what I hoped to hear this morning. And, truth to tell, I was in no mood myself to have to referee a slanging match between two colleagues.

As I pondered on whether this dispute, whatever it was, was going to disrupt our development schedule, John Chivers, one of we three laughing cavaliers, came in removing his topcoat.

"Morning - got to get a coffee," he said "I'm in the dog house, Mary doesn't like me anymore."

Mary, his wife, was the most placid and tolerant person I knew, so what John had done to get that response must have been pretty bad.

"Sorry about that, what happened?"

"You tell me." he said disappearing into the kitchen.

I raised a quizzical eye to Susan and decided to leave well enough alone. My main concern was the project, and it had to be done regardless.

As the morning progressed the atmosphere didn't get any better and it wasn't long before bickering turned to argument and argument turned to threats. Stephen resorted to smoking again and could be seen in his office puffing away with the distinct look of someone who once had a lot of self esteem, but now despised himself for allowing others to see that he was at a loss to find a solution to the dilemma.

I tried my best to placate each man and point out the stupidity of it all. It wasn't that Martin and Stephen had fallen out, it was that each man respected the other enormously but simply couldn't define what it was that had divided them. Neither could apologise because they hadn't a clue what to apologise for.

As for me, I was getting short tempered too. John was lethargic and gave the impression that all the antagonism that Martin and Stephen were expressing was making him feel deeply insecure and, as such, he was getting threat sensitive. Twice he snapped back at me when I made a simple request for more data and I, in turn, told him to "get a bloody grip." which was definitely the wrong thing to say.

By the end of the day all of us were wound up like clock springs and even Cathy had taken Stephen's wrath when he failed to find some invoices that should have been directly at hand. "You're the friggin admin' officer," he shouted, "what's the point of you administering if everything is as chaotic as it would have been if you weren't here!" A wholly unfair remark because Cathy did the work of three and never complained.

Cathy didn't cry, or make any retort, she simply didn't appear the next day.

I found that out as I entered the office that morning and found Susan being consoled by John and Martin.

"Jesus, what now?" I asked.

"Susan has quit - Cathy says she's had enough too. She's going in to see Stephen when he arrives." John and Martin had clearly made some effort to convince Susan to reconsider, but even they gave the impression that if she did actually go they might follow her.

Now, I would be the first to admit that I suspected foul play in all this. Even in my rather weary and befuddled state, I was still able to appreciate that the firm was on the slippery road to a complete collapse if things continued as they were and I suspected a competitors hand in it. Oh yes - we had competition in our sector, and one or two competing outfits weren't above slipping a spanner in our works if that's what it took to get the edge on a big contract.

As I pondered on this Stephen suddenly shot out of his office looking at me with much less fondness than I would have liked.

"It would be nice if some bloody work got done around her, I might remind you that if we don't complete the current contract we are all out of a job - and that means you too Susan."

It was the end of the line for Susan and her hackles went up. "Don't you dare speak to me like that Stephen - you've driven Cathy out and I'm following suit - I resign!"

Stephen froze in the doorway of his office his face contorting with frustration.

"Good, you aren't indispensable - not Cathy, nor you, nor anyone else. See if I damn well care!"

Stephens door slammed shut as he threw all his weight against it.

The icy silence that followed was only broken by a short sob from Susan as she pulled on her coat and ran out of the main door. In the aftermath of the confrontation I could do nothing more than sit down in Susan's chair and dig in my pocket for another aspirin, hoping that three of them might have some effect.

I felt awful and had no inclination to respond to John and Martin's hang-dog expressions. In theory we should have been tackling some difficult engineering problems, instead we were behaving as though waiting for the pronouncement of a death penalty. And, in a sense, we were - the firm was already dead and there seemed little that could be done to resurrect it.

As I sat there wondering if I should simply make a run for it and go home, a blue-overalled individual carrying two large boxes walked into the office.

"Morning - I'm your area service technician for your new vending machine, is it functioning okay? We always check after a few days, the failure rate is often very high in the first four weeks. After that, it levels out and can mean ten years of trouble free operation. We don't want our customers unhappy because the machine doesn't give satisfactory results, so here I am."

He smiled, an ingratiating smile tinged with a certain shyness.

"No," I grumbled, "it seems to be all right, but you can check it. I suspect we won't have it much longer anyway."

He made no reply to this statement but put down the two cardboard boxes and looked around to see where he should go.

"There, in the kitchen." I pointed at the kitchen door and with a nod of thanks he disappeared.

I was still coping with a pounding head when he returned.

"Yes, well - all seems okay. I notice you consume a lot of coffee."

"Indeed we do," I said "tons of it - well... we did!"

"Right he said, while I'm here I'll top up the coffee and powdered milk storage bins."

"Why not, right to the top." I quipped sarcastically.

"Certainly," he replied, "I notice your machine was loaded with de-caffeinated coffee - bet that calmed you all down. From what I heard from the installation crew, it seemed everyone here was permanently addicted to caffeine and was constantly on a high. Want to stay as you are with the de-caff' or would you prefer to get your hourly fix - it's all the same to me!"

Inner Pickle

My firm in Holland had sent me back to London to arrange a visa for an engineering project in Saudi Arabia. Being a British national, my visa had to be processed in the UK.

My wife and I were living in Eindhoven, at the time, so I had to fly in from Schipol to Heathrow and twiddle my thumbs and toes while the Saudi embassy took their time in processing the visa application.

Being stuck in a hotel for a couple of days gave me the chance to unwind and enjoy a leisurely schedule while things were resolved. The Croydon hotel was comfortable and the food good so, apart from a constitutional walk in the morning and late afternoon, I entertained myself by reading sci-fi novels and flirting with the female staff (don't tell my wife!).

It was while I was sitting down for dinner on the first night of my arrival that I remembered that I had a golden opportunity to buy a few things that were unobtainable in Holland. The thing was that the range of UK products available in the Dutch supermarkets was limited, and so we missed simple things like HP Sauce, the complete Heinz range and a variety of tinned goods like processed peas, 'Cuppa Soups' and the like.

My wife was particularly partial to a sandwich spread called Branston Pickle, but it was impossible to find it in either Dutch, German or Belgian shops - we know, we tried!

Although my wife had said nothing about it when I left for the UK, I had a feeling she would be delighted if I brought back a present of her favourite relish.

Strange to relate, the hotel where I had taken a room was somewhat distant from any central shopping area or a supermarket. The hotel and its surroundings essentially made up an urban sprawl, and even with my longish constitutional ambles, I saw very few shops.

It was only when my exploration of the area took another direction that I came across a retail cash and carry. It wasn't big, but I suspected it would contain all that I wanted.

I had to sign in as a temporary member of the store but with formalities over I was free to wander up and down the aisles, looking at all the things I should have bought, but couldn't because there was no way I could get everything shipped back to Holland.

As it was, I came across the target item as I meandered around the delicatessen displays. There, in splendid regimentation, was stacked every known brand of sauce, relish and condiment ranging from ten brands of barbecue mustard to the original Worcester sauce and five competing rivals.

What I wanted was Branston Pickle and at first it was invisible. Then, to my dismay, I was confronted not with a variety of Branston jar sizes but just one - a one gallon catering size.

Now this was not what I wanted - first it was more than I needed and second I was very unsure about transporting a gallon of Branston pickle through two airports and an intervening air flight. But then, it was Hobson's choice, and as I sized up the dimensions of the glass jar I began to suspect it was feasible - it would have to go as hand luggage!

I returned to the hotel using both hands to hold on to the pickle jar and received some very curious looks from the staff as I walked in through the foyer and into the lift. Nevertheless, for all the embarrassment I endured I had my prize and was looking forward to presenting ten years worth of Branston Pickle to my wife. I anticipated an amazed look on her face when I showed it to her.

But how to carry it?

My small holdall, packed with my change of clothes, would not do and anyway it would be in flight baggage and out of my protection. What I did have was a leather briefcase that opened at the top like the mouth of a shark. There was little in it and all the documents and papers not immediately needed during my journey could be slipped in to a side pouch. As hand luggage, I could carry it on to the plane. Only my umbrella occupied any space in it and so I stretched the case open to its limit and, with the advantage of a slippery glass surface, forced the jar of pickle down. To my relief, and with millimetres to spare, it slipped in to nestle comfortably at the bottom of the briefcase. I applied maximum pressure to the two sides of the case and latched the overlapping strap to close it.

It looked as though the case was eight months pregnant, but I had no qualms about that. The first problem was solved - the next was getting it back to Eindhoven in one piece!

The trip to Heathrow was uneventful - I hardly noticed the oversized briefcase as I carried it into the departures section of the terminal and was able to book in without any fuss. Having no reason to stay back, I decided to get all the security formalities out of the way and get into the departure lounge and have a look at the duty free shops.

I was part of a very small queue and was soon faced with the metal detectors and baggage X-Ray conveyor.

I emptied my keys, pens and other metallic objects into the 'trinkets tray' before passing through the metal detector. I was then expecting to be searched by a security officer but instead I was confronted by two of them.

"Please take your items and your briefcase to the desk over there sir."

They both stayed to my front like a human gate - the only direction I could take was the one they were indicating.

I quickly returned my 'trinkets' to my pockets and picked up my briefcase from the end of the X-Ray conveyer.

I approached the long desk indicated, behind it, stood a uniformed security officer. Strangely, as I approached, he moved further back behind the desk. As I placed my briefcase onto the counter, I felt the instant presence of bodies to my left and right and as I looking up and around I found myself sandwiched by two very large police officers. The really uncomfortable side of this event was not that they were there, but the fact that their Heckler and Koch sub-machine guns were pointing at me!

"Would you care to tell me what's in the case sir." said the man behind the desk in a voice that was obviously having trouble being kept under control.

"Only Branston Pickle and my umbrella." I replied, fairly sure that my robust answer would convince them that I definitely wasn't whatever they thought I was.

I detected a slight snort of disdain from my uniformed companion on the left but the other two seemed stunned into silence by my remark.

"Open the case sir." said the security man at long last.

As I moved forward to unlock the safety strap of the case, I felt the two officers to my left and right pressing me even closer.

As the strap snapped back and the two sides of my briefcase gaped open (almost with an audible sound of relief) I was forcibly frozen in position by the two men standing by me. The security officer leaned forward tentatively and looked into the case.

After a very short interval, his head came up and he laughed.

That laugh broke the tension, and my two custodians both sniggered as the security man tipped my bag forward so that they could see inside.

"Bloody hell," I heard, "Branston bloody pickle."

"Oh yes," I said to the security man "what did you think it was?"

He smiled and beckoned me over behind his counter. I was suddenly divested of my well-armed escorts who disappeared as if they had never been there. As I was freed,

I managed to close my bag (much more easily - it was well used to its contents now) and followed in the direction the security man was going.

We walked a short distance so that we were behind a partition screening the X-Ray machine. I saw two operators viewing TV screens and I watched as ghostly images passed into view as on the other side passengers were being screened.

My security man then went to another screen and pressed a button on an instrument panel. The TV screen suddenly brightened into life and on it was a picture.

"You can see why we stopped you sir, your umbrella and your pickle jar under X-Ray radiation give an almost perfect impression of either a bomb or a short barrelled rocket launcher. There was no way we could let you through without a thorough check."

"I had to agree, it was uncanny, the ghostly outline of the jar appeared to be a big magazine, the umbrella end protruding out like the end of a barrel. Furthermore the angled handle seemed like a pistol grip.

"I'm sorry, I had no idea that this is how it would be seen." I said, and hoped I could escape the whole embarrassing situation as soon as possible.

"I suppose you think me stupid for carrying Branston Pickle around in my briefcase, but there's a very good reason for it." I said.

"Not at all sir," he smiled, "last week we had a sales rep come through carrying perfume samples in metalised egg-like bottles - we thought they were grenades. But, that was nothing compared to the fellow we stopped recently. He was due to go on a hiking holiday, his bag had three spare gas cylinders for a portable stove. Effectively small bombs"

"Oh - so I'm not quite at the top of the list?" I quipped.

"No sir, not yet, but I would remind you that if the aircraft you are due to fly in suddenly lost cabin pressure, your jar would probably explode! However, we can't stop you on that supposition."

With that joyous remark my encounter with the airport security ended. When I finally got back to our flat in Eindhoven my wife was surprised and delighted as I extracted the jar from my briefcase and handed it to her.

"Goodness, didn't you find it difficult carrying it through the airport, I imagine it wasn't easy."

Not wishing to admit that I had in fact been literally in a pickle on the way out of Heathrow, I decided to say nothing.

"No, not a problem." I said hoping to deflect any more on the subject.

"Well, all I can say is you were lucky - as you came in I thought you had a bomb in your briefcase - good job no one else thought so!"

Serves You Right

Tennis was never my forte' - I'm far too short, wide of shoulder and suffer from severely foreshortened arms. Mark you, my simian upper torso has no disadvantages when it comes lifting a scotch or two. But as far as tennis goes, I can hardly stroke a racket properly, let alone volley an accurate ball down the court. Give me an opponent with anything like a normal physique, and a modicum of experience, and I have lost before I start.

My wife Silvia on the other hand is not bad at all - she has a lithe, athletic body, a very firm grip and a tendency to move around the court like a scolded cheetah.

For all my tennis ineptitude I spend a lot of time down at the tennis club, not necessarily to play or support my wife, but because they have an excellent well subsidised bar.

Now you might think that you've heard all this before - disaffected husband props up club bar while wife has a passionate affair with tennis coach. Well, it wasn't quite like that! Quite the reverse really, and when I think back, I'm still astonished it happened.

It was a beautiful, late spring, morning and Silvia was ready for the off. She had a match, supposedly with one of the other male club members and she was doing her best to hurry me up so she could get an hour at the club with the tennis ball launcher. She preferred to limber up against a machine - she claimed it was more demanding than a human player and didn't argue about line faults.

Of course she had a point - who was I to contradict, especially since she had informed me that I was banned from watching her court warm-up's or games (my presence thereby cramping her style!).

While she demolished her opponent, I was expected to vanish into the clubhouse until her one incognito 'after game' drink was consumed; after which I was summoned for the drive home.

Truth is, on both counts I was delighted at her attitude and so, on the morning in question, I said my goodbyes and good lucks to her at number three court's battered entrance gate.

As I made my way back to the clubhouse I heard the launcher start to blow balls. Moments later came the answering thwack from my wife's racket as she pummelled them into the high chain-linked fencing which enclosed the court.

I was really looking forward to a double scotch (well, it was way past eleven a.m.!) and I literally bounded into the bar already digging for my wallet and extracting one of the three twenty pound notes I had secreted there when Silvia wasn't looking.

I was in luck, the bar was poorly patronised with only a smattering of members imbibing their morning tipples. As I approached the bar the whisky guzzling, permanently stoned, club secretary sidled up to me from a small gaggle of 'don't play, can't play' inmates further down the bar.

"Hello Nigel you old sod," he slurred, "didn't think you were still up to a game - good for you...but you'd best not guzzle too much of the ol' hooch you know, it'll screw up your st'... stamina."

Just for a second I was startled by his inebriated remark, and then it dawned on me that he had mistaken my name for Silvia's on the court-booking list. The list was always published on the club notice board the day before the actual matches.

"Hello Jimmy, you've mistaken me for Silvia, I'm not playing today."

"Are you... s'not?" my already sozzled club secretary slurred,

"Damn sure I saw you down as being matched to Mrs. Cantwell - I'll just go an' look."

With that he negotiated a rather unsteady pirouette and marched away with a decided list to starboard.

I was in no way concerned, and after a brief and loud 'hail fellow, well met' with the friendly barman, I managed to sink one good-sized scotch before Jimmy reappeared.

"It's true - your playin' Ed'... Edwina Cantwell in an hour on number four."

He almost fell in to me as he executed a slight bow of self-congratulation and came upright, smiling a smile of malicious glee.

"Sh'... She's good yu' know - almost made women's county champion year before last. Only gave up comp'... competitive playing recently."

By this time I was getting a little irate and waved to the barman for a refill.

"Listen, I don't care what you think you saw on the match listing, I never put myself down for a game this morning, it's an error, and I am certainly not playing - regardless of whether its Mrs. Cantwell or the bloody prime minister."

"Ooo - methinks Nigel is getting cold feet," he said, exhaling a vapour vaguely approaching the effect of Sarin nerve gas, "Edwina's going to be truly miffed with you and she has a lot of influence in the club you know - you and Silvia are going to be *persona non grata* if you ain't careful."

He smiled another sardonic smile and gave me a bleary eyed wink as he turned and waddled away.

God, I was in a corner - I had some kit with me but I was in no condition to play a hard game against a woman who revelled in competitive games. And yet, if I didn't there was a good chance that this Mrs. Cantwell would use her influence to block each of our reinstatements of club membership. This was one of the few clubs in the area where membership was renewed each year based on a vote by the club's committee. Personally, I was indifferent to the tennis and much of the club's other activities but Silvia wasn't - if I were shown to have prevented her from maintaining her club status, life would be hell!

Okay, I thought, I'll play this silly bitch and lose as fast as possible. After all, I'm making no claim as a competent player - what difference does it make if she thrashes me in straight sets or I fight her long and hard and still lose. All I needed was a serviceable racket and my somewhat musty kit, which was long unwashed and crammed into the boot of the car. I would change, borrow a racket, and scramble down to number four court, where I would surrender the match with pleasure. Immediately I was vanquished, I would head back to the bar.

I found an old racket in the changing rooms and although the strings were a bit slack I was sure it was well up to losing a match. I changed hurriedly and put my trust in some aerosol deodorant to subdue the distinct odour coming from my white top and jock strap. At least my shorts appeared to be relatively clean, and with that realisation a slightly higher degree of confidence took over. I departed the changing rooms and skipped down to court four, all the time promising myself the double scotches I was going to treat myself to after the impending ordeal with the undoubtedly odious, and repulsive, Mrs. Cantwell.

As I negotiated the access pathway and arrived at my destination, court four was entirely vacant! And to my horror, I realised as I stood in the middle of my court that I was also standing behind the dividing fence of court three - where a distinctly familiar female form had her back to me.

Christ - it was Silvia!

Her male partner was distracted by the game and for the moment at least gave no indication of recognition.

I was about to have a minor panic when a voice floated towards me in the court from the other side of the net.

"Are you Nigel - I'm Edwina, thanks so much for agreeing a match. I have so much trouble getting a game these days - no other member will play me - they tell me its because they don't want to be humiliated. I can't understand it."

As I looked round I was suddenly overcome with lust.

Mrs. Edwina Cantwell was absolutely stunning. She had a figure to die for and her almost Grecian features and blond hair gave her all the appearance of an Aphrodite. She had very similar features to Silvia, only this Mrs. Cantwell had much more of everything.

I almost dropped my racket in astonishment and felt my mouth dry up as I attempted to offer an appropriate reply. Instead, all that came out was a slight vocal squeak and a cough; I was already doing badly!

To cover my embarrassment I raised my racket and smiled, reluctantly moving over to the reverse side of the net that her voluptuous body now occupied.

"I'm not in your league." I laughed unconvincingly "Please be kind to me, I'm a bit out of practice."

"It's okay," she replied with a smile, "I'm a bit rusty too."

As she lifted her racket and volleyed the ball away to begin the warm up, I began to think I'd heard a voice like hers before, but for the life of me I just couldn't identify it.

I was still puzzled as I instinctively, and without much in the way of expectation, returned the shot. Good

107

luck was with me, I dropped it directly in front of her and she stepped back for the return.

And so it went - from warm up to the first game of the first set - and as play developed I was surprised at my failure to be a failure! She placed her serves and returns well, but I was always able to make a game of it, sometimes even demonstrating a touch of athleticism. We were twenty minutes into the match when I noticed two bodies standing outside the court fencing watching us play. As I attempted an overhead volley, which ordinarily would have escaped me, I had the exhilarating experience of executing a perfect and powerful shot, so positioned that Edwina just stood still as it rocketed past.

I was basking in the sheer pleasure of having once performed an ideal shot when I heard the clapping. It was the two individuals standing outside the court. As I turned to look, I saw that one of them was Silvia, the other the clubs seeded number two, a guy called Emmanuel. He was fair, tall and handsome, the epitome of all that I considered nature should have endowed on me - I hated his guts!

"Very nice, why didn't you ever play me like that?" Silvia said.

I was going to offer a riposte about what the opponent allowed you to do, when I noticed how close Silvia was to Emmanuel - God help me, they were holding hands!

I was taken aback I confess, but my sudden confidence on the court gave me a touch of self-assurance, so I strolled over to where they were. As I did so I caught sight of Edwina coming in the same direction.

"What's this Silvia - I can't believe you would be so bloody blatant in making a cuckold of me - you never allowed your sordid activities to become public before."

She smiled, and truth to tell it was a sympathetic smile.

"I'm sorry Nigel, but you see I had to arrange a way for you to vacate our marriage with dignity and with less bitterness than otherwise."

That remark had me well stunned - if ever there was a blow to my vanity that was it. Not only was she telling me that my marriage was at an end, the woman was implying that giving me notice by a tennis court, with her lover in tow, was a way of salvaging my dignity and misery.

That twisted logic was just about the limit - I was livid.

"How dare you," I blustered, "you have the audacity to stand there and..."

I was just about to lift my racket and drive it onto the fence behind which my radiant looking wife and lover were hovering, when I heard Edwina speak.

"Nigel - let me explain."

I looked to my right and Edwina was facing me.

Now I knew where the familiarity came from - that voice was a voice from my past. Edwina wasn't Edwina, she was Elena, Silvia's sister.

God, it was at least eleven years since I last met her and even then it was during the sadness of her husbands funeral. All I remembered was that she had been draped in black and inconsolable. I'd had the fleeting chance of offering my condolences and over a few short minutes was able to express genuine pity for her utter devastation.

"Okay, what's this all about?" I asked. "I remember you now Elena...you owe me an explanation."

Elena came closer to me.

"We're sorry it had to be this way Nigel, but Silvia is in love with Emmanuel - she wants a divorce. She knows how unhappy you have been over the last five years but has no malice towards you. She decided that the best way out was simply to play a game of tennis... I mean mixed doubles, where one of the partners exchanges sides every set. I've been on my own and lonely for a long time now. Silvia knew I found you decent and attractive so I agreed to take her place - that is if you agree to it. I simply become Silvia for the duration. After all, we are very similar."

It was true, they were - but I was flabbergasted by the suggestion.

"Don't be so silly," I said, "everyone knows Silvia by sight and this simply won't work, and even if it could, what makes you think I would fall in with it?"

Emmanuel, now with the impertinence of having his arm around my wife's waist, started to reply, but Silvia interjected.

"It's either that or a very messy divorce Nigel - neither of us can afford it - financially or emotionally."

"Oh yeah, and the alternative you and Elena have cooked up is a better option? Legally it's a minefield." I opined.

Silvia looked hard at me.

"No! Elena knows exactly what she is getting in to and I'm sure you and her will bond - after all, neither of you would be here by choice - I'm sure you would eventually find other forms of recreation, so your disappearance from the club wouldn't be missed. Outside of this environment you are just another couple."

I looked at Elena and had to admit that she stirred my hormones appreciably. Nevertheless, I had definite doubts it could work - and how in hell would Silvia pull it off. She was a known quantity.

"I can't see that we have a hope - regardless." I said. "Elena would be living with a stranger - it might not work."

Elena glanced at Silvia and smiled knowingly.

"I'm very willing to try," Elena said "you strike me as kind and considerate. I have no unrealistic ambitions and anyway, I appreciated your kindness all those years ago and I'm already fond of you even after a few minutes on the court."

I had to admit the temptation was enormous but I remained doubtful.

"Thank you, but the chances remain slim - I don't think you have worked this out."

"Yes we have, Silvia said, talking earnestly through the fencing, "I've been preparing this for a long time Nigel, and it will work."

I shrugged, I was unconvinced and felt torn between what I would like to happen, and what I thought would happen.

As I briefly pondered on the dilemma, Jimmy the club secretary came into sight, still slightly the worse for his mid- morning boozing with his cronies. We all waited impatiently for him to pass us by but instead he stopped and came abreast of Silvia and Emmanuel.

"Good game everyone - I trust all's well?"

We acknowledged with a few grunts and I was hoping for a quick dispersal so I could discuss things with Elena.

However, all my doubts vanished when Jimmy turned to Silvia and with laborious articulation said "Good to see you here Mrs. Cantwell, I see your partner is keeping you at match fitness... I take it we will be seeing a lot more of you and Mr. Cantwell here - sorry... too formal... I mean Emmanuel, the club's esteemed number two." He grimaced a tipsy smile and then, peering through the fence, he took a second to focus on me "Good Lord here's Nigel... and my goodness I see your wife is here too." He turned slightly to address Elena, "Silvia... if I may be so bold... welcome. I'm Jimmy, club secretary - forgive my manners... I can't greet you properly through this fence - incidentally, can I buy you all a drink?

I smiled at Elena - Silvia was right, it would work.

So... You Want to Be an Inventor?

So you want to be an inventor - a total success? So did I!

My idea for getting lots of loot was unique (and if not unique, then pretty clever!).

Why it occurred to me wasn't all that surprising really, since I had to live with my old dog Joe.

Joe was a worn out Boxer who farted obnoxious gases just as much as he dumped huge amounts of hair all over my flat. What I needed, and God knows all other owners of mangy dogs needed, was a method to reduce canine flatulence and a way of stopping them from shedding hairs and fluff everywhere. I decided that the hair problem should be tackled first (truth to tell, there was more hair than stench. Indeed, so much hair was getting into my food that I was becoming constipated with hair balls. Either Joe went or the hair did!

It was a simple concept - it came to me that if hair lacquer holds hair together, maybe something similar would stop it falling out!

Well, the technical side wasn't so difficult - I simply used my ole' granny's Victorian recipe. A little gum Arabic and flour diluted in a solvent of water and alcohol and then heated until slightly glutinous.

It sure was sticky!

I bought enough of the ingredients to fill three thousand clear spray bottles. These I purloined as 'seconds' from the local plastics factory (who made them for plant spraying) and I was away! Jack, my mate from the pub, was foreman in a printing works and he printed out the labels. I wrote the blurb -

HAIRSTOP !

The Guaranteed Way to Stop Pet Hair Spreading
Just Spray a light coating of HAIRSTOP over the back and hind quarters of your Pet and not only will hairs be a thing of the past but your canine pal will scratch less. Your pet will enjoy a sterile coat and will need much less grooming. More Importantly, your home and food will remain hair free for at least a week. Use HAIRSTOP once a day (or twice during moulting) and you'll never need to worry about a hair and flea infested home again!

God, what an idea! Technically simple and comercially as good as it gets! I made each bottle for seven pence and sold them for... well, that at first was the problem!

Nobody knew me you see - after all, the label didn't exactly say 'Unilever', 'Du Pont' or some other well advertised and famous manufacturer on it - so most of the pet shops were naturally wary of taking on a product that didn't have a big reputation behind it. Someone said that nobody would buy it without some kind of liability insurance - or other legal protection - behind the product, I knew then that I had to think again!

But bloody hell, lots of pet owners out there were surely screaming for a product like this!

Okay, (I decided) let's see if we can find all the suckers and add a little commercial pressure to the retailers - a little advertising would be certain to get the mugs asking for it and then the subsequent distribution to the pet shops would be easy.

I remember that the ad' went into the papers on a Thursday - not a large ad' (admitted) but then, I was a little short of cash. Oh yes, and it wasn't one of the nationals, just a local rag (but good circulation I was assured).

Results were, as they say, a little disappointing.

My next round of the pet shops left me with the profound feeling that my marketing efforts had been a waste of time – the ad' hadn't elicited a single enquiry. 'Ask at your pet shop for HAIRSTOP' might just as well have read 'Ignore this advertisement if you see it'! However, someone did mention that if I was going to advertise, why not make it mail order and cut out the middlemen (that is the pet shops) altogether. So then I could avoid liability problems, people wouldn't ask if it were made by a reputable firm because it would be too late by the time they got it, and if people weren't satisfied they could send it back for a refund - to a fictitious address that is! This was, in a word, splendid! And, (to a certain extent that is), it worked. The second advertisement, this time inviting people to order by mail, resulted in seventeen orders. (though, strangely, two were from pharmaceutical companies!). Still, things were moving, and by the first week I had cleared a grand total of 112 bottles of HAIRSTOP and could see a day when I would be operating at a profit!

Week two and the turnover with advertisement number three reached 720 bottles; I was obviously becoming a success. Mark you; there was the odd worry - like the letter from the crazy old bat who said her Pekinese cracked when it moved. There were others too, like the man whose letter started with an profanities, moved on to a series of persistent expletives and ended with a decidedly nasty obscenity. There were threats 'to do me in' if they ever got hold of me and six small minded customers actually complained that their post arrived all glued together - what did they want for £3.50 plus p&p! One letter, (was it trading standards?) even mentioned 'licensing, product evaluation and testing' but I didn't understand that bit. So, things were looking up.

Time to get serious!

I needed to ensure that what looked like a nice little number was not going to get pirated by some big combine looking for a mug to sucker. Being slightly less than a pratt was the essence of good business so I decided to patent the idea while I had some cash. What the hell - patent pending, written on the bottle, was going to make all the big boys think twice - and if I registered the brand name 'HAIRSTOP', I would also get a bit of insurance against nicking a soon-to-be household word.

Charley Bennett, another drinking pal of mine, had once been a solicitor's clerk. After lubricating him with a few brews he agreed to get the patent things moving and promised to get back to me in a few days. Once again... splendid!

Getting premises for the large-scale production of the 'hair glue' wasn't a problem - all right, the old workshop was close to the waste vats of the sausage factory and the all pervading and appalling stench made it cheap to hire. But these were trivial problems, in the winter it wasn't too bad, and I knew that the alcohol vapour and the gum Arabic stewing in my vats would mask the smell of rotting entrails over the summer months! I hired a couple of down-and-outs to mix the ingredients and fill the bottles. Their biggest problem was licking and sticking on the labels, but this was resolved when I told them to use the residue of the vats as an adhesive.

Advertisement four was bigger. This time in a national tabloid using a layout that was really eye-catching. The post flooded in and I had a hell of a time getting enough newspapers to wrap up all the bottles (I keep costs DOWN!). In the end I had to admit defeat and gave up trying to write return addresses on my betting slips and sticking them on the parcels with the vat dregs. I had to get professional! Larry at the chip shop was very obliging – for a backhand tenner he let me have a thousand sheets of white wrapping paper and suggested that if I was short of ways to address the parcels why not tear off the return address on the orders and stick them on! Yeah, Larry always could see the quick solution!

The next day Charley Bennett turned up. He wanted to write what he called the 'specification' - though what the hell that was I couldn't fathom. He asked me to give him the recipe for the product and then pointed out that I stood no chance of getting a patent unless I disclosed the 'inventive step'. I must admit to being somewhat chary on this but realised that either I trusted him or I didn't; and since no other sod was going to be my agent for anything less than a couple of grand, I might as well dive in. It only took a few minutes to lead him through the ingredients list and the heating process, and the matter was done. He made a few notes, doodled on a couple of forms, looked again at the blurb he had written and then asked for a share of the business if the patent came through and he undertook to handle the finances for me.

Hell! He didn't want much did he?

I told him to take a hike, but promised to pay for the postage etc. He said he would be around again soon to complete the trade name registration forms.

When I got back to the office I had two irate customers to fend off. It was clear that some of the threatening letters were genuine. One guy, with what looked like a skinned rabbit on a lead, said his dog needed a vet to cut away its coat after 'HAIRSTOP' was applied. The dog had rolled in builder's sand and the spray had formed a concrete-like layer impossible to remove. The other nitwit claimed his dog had rubbed its paws over its eyes and was now as blind as a bat after the eyelids got glued down to the fur. I made the mistake of sniggering when I recalled the tale of the 'winky-wanky bird' whose eyelids were stitched to his foreskin. This did not please the two dog-lovers and just before they were about to lay in to me I beat a hasty retreat and got my two factory down-and-outs to throw them off the premises.

It was while I was hiding in the workshop that I noticed that the stock of methyl alcohol was only a third what I expected. It looked as if my employees were getting well lubricated at my expense. When they came back I fired them and went looking for some more cheap help. No luck - it looked as if the word was out among the local vagrants and in a moment of feigned bon - homi, I re-hired my delinquent staff of two on condition that they didn't consume the stock. I promised a bottle of hooch every Friday if they kept their word. They mumbled their agreement and I was back on course again.

Time passed and output remained steady. Good enough for me to begin to plan expansion. The only fly in the ointment was the conspicuous absence of Charley Bennett. I didn't expect much from him but having given him a chance to escape his alcoholic haze I was more than disappointed. After this one flash of silly sentiment I forgot about it and pressed on.

It must have been about 12 months later that things started to go wrong. Out of the blue, the post brought a great thick wad of papers - it appeared to be a summons to defend a class action by 52 people, all of whom had bought my marvellous HAIRSTOP and were suing me for the physical and psychological trauma caused to their pets.

Next day I was visited by the Trading Standards and the Health and Safety people who gave me notice that they were closing me down on at least two hundred counts of contravening working practices and supplying 'a noxious substance for gain'.

Later, as I licked my wounds in my office, my eye happened to glance toward a newspaper advertisement, which from the drawing of a hairy dog clearly rang a bell! I couldn't believe it - this was a product from a well-known company specialising in pets and their new offering was called STOPHAIR!

This, as the advertisement revealed, was an innovative and well-tested formulation now subject to a Patent application. Unlike previous products it was chemically well constituted ensuring that the application was effective without 'risk of permanent adhesion, damage to eyes or degrading to an impossibly tacky residue. Our product dries rapidly' it said

Next morning, nursing a very bad hangover, I phoned the contact number given in the advertisement and asked to speak to the marketing manager handling the sales of 'STOPHAIR'.

A very nice lady said that the manager wasn't in but Mr. Bennett would call back if I left them my number.

I numbly left my office number and was so immersed in my troubles that I almost didn't twig. It was only after the phone rang about twenty minutes later that I recognised the voice of my old pal Charley and his words confirmed my worst fears.

When he heard me croak out my protestations at his treachery he had enough compassion to gently point out that all was fair in love and intellectual property. I should have ensured that he operated under a confidentiality agreement, had been retained exclusively for 'the benefit of the inventor and/or its company', and was promised a fair remuneration.

Without any of this, he said, I had given away my rights and even if I were to complain to the Patent Office it was unlikely I could prove anything. Furthermore, I couldn't afford a civil action in the courts, not least because I was (a) bankrupt (b) about to go to prison and (c) his company could hold up the process for years slowly draining me of my spirit and any cash I had left. In short, he said, I was a mug and in this life 'one never gave a sucker an even break'!

It took a long time to recover from my hard lessons.

Two years passed before I got out of prison, got straight and saw Charley again; and only then did I realise that I was better - better because I managed to control the fury that I usually experienced every time I thought of him. Even seeing him in his new Jag and business suit, knowing that his company had made millions from STOPHAIR, in the interim distributed to satisfied pet owners all over the world, simply left me empty but no longer enraged.

However, what really rankled was the two guys who stopped me as I left the prison gates and gave me a fiver – I'm sure they looked like cleaner, and better fed versions, of the two down-and-out's I'd hired to work in the factory!

One day I suppose I'll get even. But even if I don't I may yet turn my experience to advantage - I have been experimenting with old Joe my Boxer, I have succeeded in making his farts smell vaguely like rose hip syrup - next step, roses themselves!

Jenny's Guilt

The Whitechapel murders had stopped.

The fear that had hung like a clinging, all pervading, miasma over the filth encrusted warren of lanes and alleys that was Whitechapel had abated, and the constant patrolling by the police had subsided into a routine patrol by a pair of Bobbies.

Now that it appeared to be safer, the street girls were beginning to show themselves in the secluded doorways, back alleys and archways, all of which served as their secluded 'back to the wall quick sixpence' parlors. The more expensive ones were now inclined to venture a little further from their rooms to attract clients. During the murders, they had taken fright and kept close to the shelter of their own front doors.

Jenny was really too old and worn out to attract much attention from the occasional 'toff ' who ventured in looking for the preteen whores. But still, every now and again, she made a shilling or two.

As things stood, she had the advantage; many of the older girls had moved away to avoid being a victim of the 'Ripper' and of late the younger ones were becoming less in evidence as many of the rich 'Johns' and other equally profitable trade moved to the west. Taken as a whole, she had much reduced competition; and it was fortunate that she did, the money she made supported a lazy son and an even lazier husband, both of whom expected her to provide the wherewithal to eat and drink.

More drink than eat.

They were a viscous pair and too often they took their frustration out on her. Not only her but others, and many a time they both came home covered in blood from some violent encounter, and would sanitize their gore covered bludgeons and knives by washing them at the courtyard pump.

The fact that these bloody incidents with her kin had peaked with the death of so many streetwalkers was no puzzle to Jenny - she knew the truth! Nevertheless, she had no suspicions about her men-folk, and even if she had, she had nothing to say to the police who had questioned her many times.

Could she inform on kith and kin - of course not.

After all, blood was thicker than water and whatever the men had done, she had more to answer for.

At her age - with only one way to make any money - reducing the competition from all the other girls significantly improved her chances of attracting trade. She had long learnt that fear of the unknown was the key - and making a murder look like the work of someone she herself could never be seen to be, gave her total security.

She had despatched five of her main rivals with total anonymity and the rest had left Whitechapel for good. She was content to simply pick up the trade they could no longer service - God willing she would never need to use the knife again - not unless Jenny the Ripper had to!

You Can't Win - You Can't Break Even
(and you can't get out of the game!)

"Buy a raffle ticket? Sir - madam?"

The overdressed and somewhat shrunken lady, lit up by her garish dress of mixed shades of yellow/orange, called out unabashed as she meandered between tables in the *'Black Cat'* cafe. "It's for cancer research - good cause," she smiled, beckoning me to dig into my purse.

"Any prizes?" I said sarcastically, "I'm hoping for something life changing. You know, I can't remember ever winning one of these raffles. "

The walking sunflower stepped closer.

"Prizes? Oh yes, but I'm afraid it will depend on the sponsors, this is a local funding drive, and the sponsors donate prizes as they will. As yet we're not sure which of the donations will be the first prize. It's either going to be a holiday somewhere exotic, or a batch of tokens to buy goods, services or entry to a recreation park... anyway, something like that."

"It doesn't really matter," I replied, "to me it's simply a donation to the charity - win or lose."

Mrs. Sunflower's arthritic fingers pulled along the edge of a perforated ticket, the top one of a thick green wad and offered it with a slightly tremulous hand.

"Claim by number," she said "winners will get notification in the local papers in about six weeks time. Good Luck,"

She took my payment and moved on to the next line of tables. With hardly a thought I folded the ticket and consigned it to a pocket in my bag, one already stuffed with receipts, tickets and miscellany.

It was many weeks time later that I had the opportunity to briefly scan a rather out of date copy of the local paper, and my eye fell on an article which recounted the a search for a raffle ticket holder, the primary winner of seven possible prizes. Although the winning ticket numbers had been published, no one as yet had claimed the prize in question. The raffle, it was reported, had been run to raise money for the cancer research fund, over and above the CRF's normal fund raising activities.

With my curiosity piqued, I started to imagine where I had secreted the ticket I had bought so many weeks ago, and after a little mental exercise of 'if I had kept it, where would it be?' I followed my hunch which led to the pocket of my handbag. I carefully laid out every piece of paper I could retrieve from my bag on the kitchen table. I flattening each and inspected the print. I was rather pleased to discover three supermarket saver tickets, and as my rather hazy arithmetic offered me the rather heady sum of £6.04 off my next grocery shop, I subsequently discovered the raffle ticket too. As I retrieved the creased and somewhat paper scrubbed ticket and examined it, to my amazement the numbers matched that given in the newspaper.

To be certain I re-read the opening paragraphs of the article and compared my ticket number with that given in the article. There was no doubt - I was the primary winner.

As a sense of glee overcame me I began to think of my prize - what could it be?

This was a red-letter day - never before had I been so fortunate - never in my whole life! I read further into the article and to my utter amazement the prestigious prize turned out to be a days driving and tuition at a racing drivers school, with the promise of being able to test drive at least three very high performance cars and additional laps in a formula 1 car.

I looked again, felt a deep tinge of regret, and then screwed up my raffle ticket and threw it into the fire.

The only consolation for me was going to be a nice hot cup of coffee - so I turned my wheelchair around, repositioned my useless legs, and disregarding my loss as only to be expected, pushed myself towards the kitchen.

Enemy's Shadow

Before I die (and young though I am, it is certain that I shall die soon) I want to tell you that I never really believed that there was an inevitable retribution or penalty for ones sins *per se*. Rather, if punishment there is, it is for being found out!

As a hired assassin the 'being found out' was followed inevitably by a rather unpalatable consequence, so I avoided it like the plague.

As far as I was concerned, being found out was to do with being sloppy and leaving a forensic trail that some bright cop could discover. I was a fast learner with a touch of luck, which ensured I missed the usual traps that inexperience laid for rogues like me, and I never ignored, or forgot, the harsh lessons of all my narrow escapes.

I learnt early on, after a good few of my competitors were banged up, that a single error or misjudgement was fatal. Only the real professionals, like me, understood the five 'P's' - i.e. Poor Planning means Piss Poor Performance. In a nutshell, carefully arranging a 'hit', and taking nothing on chance, virtually guaranteed a clean getaway, with only a statistically insignificant chance of being found out.

In short, I was good, very good, and I took any contract going.

I had no qualms. I could eliminate anyone if the price was right and there was hardly a target in the world I wasn't able to get at. Of course, I did occasionally draw the line - presidential and VIP targets were often too well guarded, and, of course, there were others - those too likely to know who the underworld professionals were for me to be able to hide my trademarks, or the secrecy of a contract. It was stupid to eliminate someone where his (or her) criminal organisation could easily establish who it was had paid for the contract, and who had carried out the hit.

Excepting those few mentioned, I was pretty well free to apply my trade to almost anyone, anywhere. It meant I travelled extensively, and not just in the US or Europe, I could tell you stories about Africa, South America and the Far East.

However, my eventual nemesis was nearer home - St. Louis, Missouri, in fact, and a far more familiar and comfortable environment than my usual overseas haunts.

The contract was an unusual one - a priest - but not your usual kind of priest. This priest was the head of a small sect that had developed on the outskirts of the city in a community normally considered to be in the lower social order. It appeared he had trodden on the toes of too many local politicians and disrupted (or maybe taken over) too many moneymaking schemes for the local patricians to ignore him any more. Trouble was, he seemed to have nine lives - every effort to thwart of frame him eventually resulted in him surviving whatever, or whoever, came up against him. It was as though he had divine protection, and his funny little band of devout followers made it known that even the anti-Christ would have no chance against the 'chosen one' who led their religious services every day.

Naturally, I was never going to believe in supernatural influence, or the existence of any earthly creature being divine or protected by God's angels. So I set about making my target's mortal life and daily movements a known quantity - discounting and disregarding any heavenly surveillance, and ensuring that my getting away from any scene of assassination, or being distant from it, was as easy as getting in to it!

126

I was selective in my choice of venue - I often preferred to make a hit look like an unfortunate accident, and why not, why attract unnecessary police interest by making the death an obviously deliberate act.

It was after watching my mark take occasional visitors to his splendid white painted chapel on the outside of town, and then, with a few of his followers, take them for the much more thrilling tour of the 'Gateway to the West' - the amazing 630 feet stainless steel archway built close to the Mississippi River downtown of St Louise - that I saw my chance.

I was already aware that the Gateway had an enclosed observation platform that visitors accessed through a series of cramped one-man lifts that took you up the full 630 feet. There was no way of accessing the outside of the Gateway, so I was stymied as regards death by an 'accidental' fall. I could however see how an unexpected heart attack in the observation platform might appear (to others at least) as the result of physical stress in the lifts.

It seemed very appropriate, so I carefully arranged to intercept the next 'church party' heading for the customary tour of the Gateway.

With a gaggle of strange faces accompanying my target, I was able to blend in fairly easily.

To the party attached to my target I was one of the visitors, to the visitors I was one of the target's party - in short the left hand was blind to the right and vice versa.

I kept myself in conversation with one or two of the visiting party, trying to be convivial but as vague and unrevealing as possible so as to mask my lack of religious sincerity. My surveillance of the sect had been reasonable informative, so that I was able to appear as a genuine, but rather shy, member of my target's congregation.

Prior to this gathering, I had only seen him at a distance, so this was the first time that I had the opportunity to see my target at close quarters and determine his character.

I had to admit, he certainly appeared to have an aura - a kind of inscrutable, if not enigmatic, power. He was able to elicit an unfathomable sense of well being among the party - even in the absence of any direct contact, I felt everyone was spellbound by his presence.

However, as I was being jostled by other visitors in the Gateway foyer, I touched him arm to arm and it was then that I become aware of the full weight of his spiritual strength. In that moment, he suddenly halted, turned and looked at me.

I froze, paralysed by a penetrating stare from an unblinking pair of black eyes. There was no discernable iris and the dark orbs seemed as infinite as space, both eyes being set into a pale, somewhat ovoid unlined face.

I find it hard to describe the effect he had on me, it was tantamount to being dropped into a refrigerator. As his fathomless black eyes locked with mine, I was suddenly gripped by an ice-cold, and overwhelming, sense of dread;

an emotion completely alien to me, and so terrifying that for a moment I lost all ability to move.

I stayed frozen to the spot for a few stretched out seconds and, as he broke his gaze and turned away from me, I found myself behind the throng of people pouring in to the Gateway. There I remained, motionless and watching the church party become surrounded by a trailing horde of other visitors.

It was now impossible to see where my target had gone, the mass of bobbing heads and moving bodies had become so dense that identifying my proposed victim was virtually impossible. Not only that, I now had no chance of discharging the vial of nicotine aerosol I had intended to release in my targets cramped lift. It was a concentrated dose, calculated to induce heart failure. Of course, an autopsy would detect the nicotine - but then, I had seen my target puffing an occasional cigar - so no suspicion would arise. However, now I had to think again!

I very quickly dismissed the effect he had on me, I put it down to a bad piece of fish my hotel had served for dinner the evening before, and after a few days I was back to my old confident self again. After a little more observation I decided that subtle tactics were not going to serve my purposes - now my mark appeared to be constantly in company with either members of his congregation or unknown individuals who seemed to arrive in droves. He was obviously popular locally and able to draw yet more interest from the congregations of surrounding churches.

No, it was time for a direct approach.

In my terms it was simple, it meant waiting for the target to be alone and then shoot him. Properly placed and contrived, and in the absence of contradictory evidence, a really well composed letter of farewell could be made to explain the sad self-destruction of a severely disturbed cleric.

I was patient to a fault - keeping the chapel under constant surveillance for a good few days and noting the comings and goings of visitors and congregations. Services appeared to end at eleven in the morning and resume at six in the evening. As the schedule repeated I became assured that the period from mid-day to three p.m. was the window of opportunity I wanted. The target was always in the chapel and at this time visitors were at their minimum.

On the day I prepared my self for the hit the weather, always unpredictable in St Louis, had turned very hot and humid. In that quite sleepy post-noon period, I made my way to the chapel along a dog-walkers path that skirted the chapel and was obscured by vegetation from the main access road.

He was in the vestry - or what served for the vestry. It was a wide extension to the rear of the chapel with heavily carpeted floors, a large oak desk, wooden cabinets and the blessing of air-conditioning.

I came through the door as quietly as possible and found him smoking a cigar and sitting in a wide, tortuously and sinuously carved Captains chair snuggled in to the desk. He heard me above the drone of the AC and skewed himself round in the chair to look at me.

I said nothing to him, indeed, there was nothing to say. I had a job to do and the sooner done the better.

Again, as at the Gateway, he locked his impenetrable eyes with mine, but I saw no fear on his impassive face. If anything there was a smirk on his lips, and his whole stance spoke of a mocking, derisive attitude.

I held my nerve and this time I was absolutely unfazed by his presence.

I brought up the .357 magnum and aimed at his head, only to discover I was incapable of pulling the trigger. Was it the same paralysis I had experienced before - a temporary loss of control brought about by his hypnotic charisma, or was it something more terrible, the inability to act because of even greater forces than I dared think of.

He stood up from the chair with a slow, snake like extension of his limbs, and walked round the desk turning to look at me.

He was my height, his shoulder length jet-black hair and dark eyes contrasted sharply with so pale a face that it gave the appearance of being powdered. He cracked a sardonic red-lipped smile, made all the menacing by a show of unusually long, and needle like, canine teeth.

"You're not the first," he said in a basso voice that even now, as I think of it, makes me shiver, "many others have tried and failed...as you will."

130

I tried to pull the trigger again only to see him scowl.

"It won't work you know - and all that you attempt is futile, though I am here in this world I am not mortal, for I am already on the other side of death."

I squawked with indignation, "Ha - not yet, but very soon - don't give me the same crap you feed your followers, I know you for what you are."

"And what am I?" he queried, standing in front of me with his legs slightly apart and his head inclined at an enquiring slant.

I told him what I thought I knew. "A charismatic charlatan - well able to attract highly impressionable followers. You tell them what they want to hear about life after death, and how obedient they must be to you, and how generous they must be to your church for it to happen...and the brainless morons believe it!"

His head drooped a little as I flung my remarks at him.

I briefly looked at my handgun, trying to see why the hammer would not respond to the trigger. It appeared to be as it always was, well oiled and in perfect working order. And yet...!

I looked back at the creature in front of me and once more saw a now indulgent smile.

"Life after death?" he said, "Do you see any graves around my chapel? Have you asked yourself why my congregation increases every day - why my fight with city hall for the erection of a bigger church is crucial for my flock, even though I have no graveyard? If not, you should."

I ground my teeth as I replied "Stick it in your crawl superman - a little hypnosis to stop me shooting you and the disappearance of people in your band of followers impresses me not one bit."

"Then it should - and you will pay for your foolishness."

As he spoke my eyes widened in astonishment. The room seemed to telescope back and to enlarge enormously. I began to shrink in proportion to the space in front of me while the view ahead dissolved into a panorama of shadows and apparitions - one overlapping the other and receding into infinity. The shadows shimmered and fluctuated, each having a slightly different profile, and each apparently thrashing for release as they struggled with the other shadows to their front and back. I heard a swelling volume of sound - voices raised in anguish, each echoing the depths of hopelessness - despairing of salvation and screaming for release. Slowly they advanced on me, forming an envelope of blackness, and I knew that unless I responded instantly I was lost to a bottomless and terrifying shadow world.

I suddenly realised that my earlier estimation of my target had been wrong - that all I believed had been too sceptical. I should have revised my approach to the hit in terms of the second possibility I had determined, and not the first.

Still, that was what the five 'P's' were about and even though I had cynically dismissed the possibility of super-natural forces, I catered for them.

Since I now found it impossible to fire the gun, I simply dropped it; at the same time pulling out the plastic container of holy water I had borrowed from the font at St Clements in town. It was a large bottle, and heavy, with it's sanctified contents all wrapped in selected pages from the bible. I had previously tested other water filled bottles to discover how easily they ruptured. However, in hope more than expectation, I hurled my heavenly missile at the enveloping black shadows streaming towards me.

There was a kind of eruption - a sound like thousands of shrieking banshees all suddenly horrified by the unexpected realisation of being sucked out of existence and having nowhere to retreat to. I watched as the water

132

burst out of the ruptured bottle, and as the page from the Bible blew away I saw the words 'Thou Shalt Have No Other God But Me!' suddenly burn brightly on the outer page and expand to huge proportions, blanketing out all the black apparitions. It all lasted less than a heartbeat, but the holy water and the forces of light had their divine effect - separating all the imprisoned souls from their black host and sending him and them into permanent oblivion.

Now I understood why he had mentioned the absence of a graveyard, and why he wanted the chapel to become a large recognized church. The bigger the congregation, the more earthly souls he could absorb, and the more he absorbed, the greater his appetite for shaping the battlefield he wanted.

Oh yes, to the dark one the earth was a battlefield he could shape to his advantage - the more souls he could take, the less there were to side with his eternal opponent - the one that strived for righteousness and virtue.

If the battlefield had been vacant, lost to the armies of men, then the war would have taken on an entirely different character. The angels and the demons would have fought it out without men as allies or enemies. Since mankind had predominantly taken the side of the saviour and the righteous, the dark one invariably fought at a disadvantage.

As I made my way from the chapel, along the circuitous route back to town and my hotel, I pondered on how it was I had managed to survive. The idea of a significant payment for my successful hit was virtually meaningless when I considered that even the 5 'P's' had hardly made it possible to stay alive - in short it had been a very close call.

The nervous tremors I had escaped with had virtually abated and now I had the sun to my back. It felt warm and comforting as I trekked back away from the church, and I almost forget the last sound I had heard as the holy water destroyed the dark one. "Beware assassin - the one above loves you not - your soul is as your shadow!" Yet I was irritated by my inability to determine the significance of this final outburst, and I was uncertain if I had heard it correctly.

I felt that whatever my recollection it was hardly something to worry about, and so I pressed on along the dog-walkers track to find my car - some distance away. It was as I came up to the car that I suddenly halted, chilled with the stark realisation that it was me who was now a marked target.

Could it be that the expedient principle - that my enemy's enemy is my friend - was never, ever, entertained in the heavenly hosts?

Could I, a killer by profession, ever be forgiven by the dark ones enemy, the lord of good, for ultimately doing good in the name of evil? Was it fair - was I to be forsaken even though I had won the battle for the righteous and had become the salvation of men?

I knew then what my destiny might be, and so a little later I decided to write down my story. I doubt it will have any credence - stories like mine seldom do. But if you are a believer in the constant and continuing war between good and evil, you might put me down as one of the contenders on the side of good, though strangely I suspect that it's this particular side that wants to see me eliminated.

Either way I have no future, for the heavenly host who see themselves as fish I am viewed as foul, and to the satanic foul, I am fish.

Evil will soon revenge it's honour and of that I am now certain - as I stand over the car's roof, writing with the hot sun behind me, I notice that my shadow has started to fade to nothing.

Wrong Place - Wrong Time!

I hadn't been in my hometown for twenty years but to my joy the old coffee shop was still in business, still trading the same old frothy pleasures it had served when last I saw it.

Okay, it had changed a bit, different faces behind the counter, a redesign of the display shelves and now, a piped music system instead of the old Wurlitzer Juke Box. Overall though the place was more or less the same as when I, a fresh faced cash strapped twenty year old, had sat for hours with my friends over a single Cappuccino. I had gone on to University, making me one of the few of the town's youth who, according to those who had an interest in it, had 'done well'.

And now I was back, on the 20th anniversary of the day I left for University; which as time passed had armed me with an engineering degree and a career. Yes, the old faces had gone and I now sat anonymous among the café's few current patrons, wholly unrecognised for who I was (except, that is, for my absent parents).

The coffee shop still smelled the same as it did and sent me back to a time when all options were open but few were well appreciated. Even the elliptical plastic tables seemed familiar, and as I sat down at the one I had always frequented and scanned the town square through the age clouded picture window I remembered so well, I saw a face I vaguely recognised crossing in front of the shop entrance.

It was a distantly familiar face, and yet I simply couldn't put a name to it, or a time when it had been

135

familiar. I thought hard to give me a reason to get out of my chair and confront the face in question, but it was not to be - not with me opening the conversation with "Hey, what's your name, it's me, how are you?"

I held back, reluctantly, and accepted the fact that I was avoiding a potentially embarrassing encounter. Yet, it was very frustrating - there he was, a man whose familiarity was so definite that I concluded that my past was far more obscure than was comfortable. How could I forget? But there it was, it was clear that my recall was faulty. Perhaps what I remembered of my days as a youth was highly selective; only the good bits? But then I reconsidered, wasn't that always the case?

It was as I sensed a slight disappointment in my quest for youthful memories that the cafe doors were flung open and the familiar face crashed in.

The face that now glared at me as recognition sunk in was no more known to me than before, but whoever he was, he certainly knew me.

I pressed back into my chair, instinctively on the defensive as he turned away from the sales counter and slowly walked towards me. The glare on his face began to transform into a mocking smile as he approached.

"It's been a very long time." he growled, "Remember me?"

I treated his intimidating query as a threat and decided not to respond. My silence only brought about another ill-mannered remark.

"You damn well should, you've been constantly around for twenty years of my life!"

I stared back, unable to identify a face that I recognised but found impossible to place. Nor could I make sense of his statement.

I had to find a way to establish who he was.

I decided to lie, it was the easiest approach and might just elicit the clue I needed.

"Yes, I know you, so now what?"

He smiled again, his dark features filled my vision while his glowering grey eyes never blinked for a second.

"I owe you something."

He leaned further down towards me and taking his hand from his jacket pocket threw a piece of folded paper on to the table.

I looked at the slightly crumpled offering but refused to take the bait and turned back to look at him again.

"What's that?" I asked.

"Why don't you find out." he retorted

I remained mystified, but if the piece of paper told me what I wanted to know then so be it. I picked up the folded sheet of paper from the tabletop and read the contents.

It was an official notice - a notice of divorce, a decree absolute between two names one of which might have rung a bell but the other was still unknown to me.

"She divorced me... I lost her... she broke my heart."

Suddenly his whole demeanour changed and as I examined the notice, he collapsed into the chair on the opposite side of the table.

"Never thought it possible that you would be here in the same place and on the anniversary of the day I met her," he croaked, "are you trying to make a fool of me?"

It was then that I knew, and my mind raced back twenty years to the last day I had met my crowd of friends in the cafe', just before going off to my fresher year at University. We had all been in loud and excited conversation and had been joined by a couple of extra faces introduced by separate members of the gang. One had brought in a friend called Marie, another a work colleague, David. For me, Marie was less than welcome. She had been a contemporary in final year at school and had a suffocating crush on me that I had found hard to deflect. Her dogged infatuation had been an unwanted distraction as I struggled with assignments and past exam papers; everywhere I looked I found her circling me like a moth around a light. This day however, I had ignored my irritation at her appearance and tried not to be unpleasant. They had both joined in the boisterous debate we usually started, and had sat on each side of me, She to my right and he to my left. I took little notice, my mind taken more on the days to come at University than the people now sitting with me and, like the rest of my friends, soon to be left behind. I spoke to both of them over the course of the time I spent saying all my goodbyes and may have detected the beginnings of a romantic engagement. She was pretty and animated; he was obviously attracted by her personality and physical charms. I introduced them to each other and left nature to take its course.

So that was it, I was being seen and blamed as the instigator of a lost love. Coincidence had compromised me. So, here I was, wrong place, wrong time. I'd come back for nostalgia. He'd come back to the café rethink and reconstruct his life. I was the last person he wanted to see.

"I'm sorry for you," I said, "I imagine I'm not the person you want to see at the moment, but you can't blame me for causing you any trouble. Your divorce has nothing to do with me. As I dimly recall I simply introduced you, someone I hardly knew, to a women who had a teenage crush on me - and that's it."

Before I had time to continue my defence, he had stood erect from his chair and towering above me interrupted my attempt at seeking absolution.

"You don't understand do you - it was your leaving that did it. As time passed familiarity bred contempt - she took me as second best and for years all I heard was your name and how much better her life would have been if she had left the cafe with you when you did. You were always the stick she beat me with - the one she yearned for in her

138

dreams. I tried - oh, how I tried. I loved her, but she never could be satisfied with me and every day I woke up with you and me in competition for her affections. In the end it was impossible - I had to escape - and yet I needed her so badly."

This I found hard to swallow - as I thought back I doubt that even in school I'd had little direct contact with Marie and apart from tolerating her constant appearances and girlish shyness, I remembered nothing of anything I did to encourage her. Yes, she never hid her obvious infatuation, but she hardly made contact during that last meeting in the café. Had I missed it? Was it because of my preoccupation with things to come? Perhaps it was, and at the time I had been entirely oblivious to her sentiments.

I had no response to his sadness, He seemed crushed by his loss and I had no genuine reply to his apparent grief except a slight sense of guilt.

I could only offer commiserations. As he slowly folded back into his chair I offered some advice I thought might console him.

"Look, it's over now, you will have to start again. You never know - perhaps she will see you in a different light now. It does happen."

He looked up from his downcast position and gave me another knowing smile.

"Oh - your so right. She did see things in another light as you put it. I went back to plead with her, but she was as spiteful as could be. I suppose I finally came to accept that she still couldn't forget you or the dream you represented."

He staggered slightly as he made to stand up from the chair again and it was then that I noticed the black-red spots on his trousers and jacket.

"She won't think about you anymore." he said with an ironic chuckle and leaned forward over the table.

"She's..."

I knew what was coming and hoped for my sake that the girl behind the counter was watching.

As I cowered back, the cafe doors were suddenly flung open and two-armed policeman raced in. My rival turned and saw the guns pointing at him.

"Too late." he said and raised his arms above his head.

Mixed Fortunes

I was in a hurry, one hell of a hurry, and finding a parking space near my dentist appeared to be impossible. I drove around for what seemed an age, with the throbbing pain of a collapsed molar stretching my concentration and patience to the limit.

On my fifth circuit, hoping to see a car leave a space, I made one last foray into the road alongside the dental surgery. I suddenly saw, through pain watering eyes, an opening in the long line of parked cars - and to my delight it was very close to the surgery itself.

I backed in quickly, but grimly aware of my physical state I was conscious not to be reckless in my attempt to get treatment. I was equally careful not to throw the car into the parking bay and add an expensive front and rear collision to my troubles. Slamming the car door behind me, I ran up the walkway to the surgery. Thankfully, I was only a few minutes late and as I confirmed my appointment with the receptionist, I was told there would be a slight delay before I could be seen.

Stoic to the last, I sat in the waiting room and endured twenty-five minutes of ever excruciating pain, watching the wall clock tick through minutes that stretched into hours.

As I sat there, wondering what was the cause of the delay, a dishevelled and angry looking individual pushed through the swing doors of the waiting room and paced quickly to the reception desk.

"Mr. Arnold," the receptionist gasped, "what happened?"

The man banged his fist on the desk "Some damn fool has taken my parking space again - surely these idiots can read - it says 'Reserved Dental Surgeon' on the sign doesn't it? Twenty five minutes I've wasted trying to park my car - dear Christ!"

Despite my miserable condition I felt obliged to own up to my indiscretion. "Excuse me," I said, still unable to articulate well through a swollen and pain racked gum, "I think I'm to blame - I was desperate - I'm in terrible pain."

He looked round at me and said "Very well, you'd better come in to my treatment room, but if you think you are in pain now wait till you see the note I've left on your car. I trust you still require treatment?"

With a sinking heart I rose to my feet, knowing that the ordeal to come was mostly of my own making.

So, that's how I came to be the 'guardian of the space' - oh, I'm not the only one. There are nine us that have a three month duty roster, taking it in turns for an hour every day to ensure the dentist's parking space is inviolate. Anyone daring to ignore our instructions are told, as we were in the note left on our cars, that they would lose their registration at the dental surgery and would not be treated anymore by 'the man'.

All things considered I was pleased to be dealt with so leniently - when I think of how appalling it would have been not to have been treated when I was, I consider my penalty rather soft. After all, it's a small town and we have only the one dental practice - the nearest otherwise is fifteen miles away.

Yet I do still wonder, fast though he was, did my dentist really have to carry out the extraction without a local anaesthetic?

Back To Front

I remember my first job well, and I distinctly remember Jack Evans the foreman of the plastics works where I spent my formative career moulding yellow plastic ducks for children's bath time. It was boring to hell and I only stuck it while I attended night school to get qualified as an industrial design engineer.

Jack Evans was no tyrant; his effervescent and lenient handling of his operators relieved the stifling repetition that we operators had to endure.

"Make sure you keep the extruder and mould temperatures at the right settings." Jack was always repeating, "Means less downtime for cleaning and (gleefully) more time for coffee breaks!"

Indeed, we revelled in the number of work breaks we enjoyed while Jack was on duty - though truth to tell we oftimes turned out ducks which were less than perfect. The quality control inspectors hardly noticed - after all, they were invariably the first to appear at the next coffee break. It began to take on an inverse pattern. We were literally having short 'work breaks' between our extended coffee sessions.

Did we care? No, we didn't!

But one day we were too engrossed in our joyous coffee and chat breaks when a short power loss caused a malfunction of all the mould temperature controllers so that they all automatically reset. With no one watching, there was no one to tell that the reset temperatures were all too high and a huge batch of shapeless ducks turned out.

Management were furious and Jack was the sacrificial lamb. They fired him on the spot for dereliction of duty and gross negligence - the rest of use were given dire 'one more transgression and you're out' warnings.

This event stayed with me for many years, leaving a sense of guilt that a man we all liked was severely penalised for what was in effect a collective irresponsibility. We should all have been fired. Yet that was never going to happen, the executive could not afford to have a completely purged workforce and a vacant factory.

Eventually I qualified and moved on, and as my career developed in polymer industrial design I took responsibility for designs ranging from computer casings to aircraft and aerospace components. As the years passed my experience led me on to develop my own consultancy, and this proved reasonably lucrative.

I arrived at *'Membury Thermo Plastics'* one spring morning after arranging a consultancy with their chief engineer the previous week. I spent a fascinating morning as they invited me to act as design consultant for the processing of a massive order for a car manufacturer. They wanted seven complex plastic sections for a new car; the mould designs being particularly intricate and tricky.

I needed to know what plant the factory had installed to determine which approach and what production level was sustainable. As I walked through the factory and all the neatly spaced extruders and moulding units, I caught a glimpse of man walking away - he had a familiar face, one I had not seen for some time and I was convinced it was Jack Evans.

I was tempted to pursue my erstwhile and regretfully lost companion, but there were things to do and if I was right about who he was, I had plenty of time to restore our friendship.

As it was, I found myself far too busy for the next week to seek him out but during one lunchtime, with the pressure off somewhat, I walked down to the shop floor and began to look for Jack. Many of the operatives had gone for lunch leaving just a few still by their machines. I approached one, a younger man. He was chair-borne, his feet cradled on an old extrusion drive with a paper on his lap. He sat munching a thick sandwich.

"I'm looking for an old friend of mine - Jack Evans, where will I find him?"

He swallowed a mouthful of sandwich.

"You won't - he's suspended."

This was no small shock, "But I saw him - last week - here on the shop floor."

"True enough," slurred the man with another bite of his mouth stretching sandwich, "Buggered up his settings again - he's due for the chop. He was suspended last week pending an enquiry. Lost too much production - the bosses won't stand for it."

I remained stunned at this news for the rest of the day unable to comprehend how Jack, nice as he was, could show so much incompetence. When he was my foreman, the one thing he wasn't was incompetent - he knew more about plastics moulding than anyone I knew. Okay, he was too easy-going with the workforce but technically he knew his stuff. So, what had happened? I decided to find out.

A day later I wondered around the lunchtime shop floor observing the nature of things and attempting to identify the area where Jack had been working. None of the machines had been shut down so it was odds on that whatever machine Jack had supervised was in no way inoperative.

I approached my earlier informant who, as was his habit, was sipping tea between large bites of a massive cheese and onion Dagwood sandwich.

"Hello again." I said.

He nodded an acknowledgement.

"Where was Jack Evan's machine before his suspension?"

"It wasn't one machine - Jack was supervisor for units ten to sixteen."

"Oh," I exclaimed thoroughly surprised "so what's this about the settings being wrong?"

"That's all I know." sandwich man said, "I don't know all the details - only what I heard."

I was even more bewildered - surely my history with Jack Evans hadn't been repeated? I had visions of Jack and his gang sitting around a table enjoying another coffee party while all around them turned into misshapen plastic ducks. Deep in thought, I meandered away and found myself standing by the monomer feed area. As I looked at the feed tubes a man walked out of the access door from the feed stock room.

"Excuse me - I don't wish to pry but do you have any information abut this problem that Jack Evans tripped up on?"

He was clearly rattled by my direct question and I could see his face become tortured with a mental struggle as he tried to decide a response.

"Who are you?"

"I'm a friend of Jack - I knew him fifteen years ago when we worked together."

"I see - well Jack's suspended - we had a special catalyst initiated thermosetting plastic shipped in for a new order - Jack said it had to be processed at a higher temperature than indicated. The exec insisted it be done as directed. Jack bowed to the front office order and set the system temperatures accordingly - but it was clear things were wrong. He tried to reset the settings but it was too late. It wasn't that we lost a batch of stock - that was nothing - it was the fact that the bloody stuff clogged up all the units from ten to sixteen. Took Jack a week to put things right. Of course, the bloody managers blamed him and he was suspended pending an enquiry. So now you know - and much good it will do your friend!"

I pondered on this bit of intelligence and decided to dig a little deeper. If what I had heard was true, Jack actually had no charge to answer, so it was simply a case of making sure that whoever was heading the enquiry Jack was to face, was presented with all the facts - at least the indisputable ones. I spent a good few days unearthing all the unpalatable evidence regarding the period prior to the arrival of the infamous co-monomer that had created the dispute, and who it was had insisted it be processed as directed in the face of objections from Jack Evans. There was little in writing regarding the order to run the batch at a specific temperature, but I compiled a lot in witness statements.

The chief engineer and I had developed a rapport and he was sympathetic to Jack Evans' plight, agreeing with me that since none of the engineering staff had been responsible for the decree that had compromised Jack Evans, it should not be his head that rolled. I handed over the compilation of evidence I had amassed and in a short time I had notification of the who, where and when of the enquiry.

As the enquiry panel convened, I waited patiently as it went through its lengthy due process. I was sipping a third cup of coffee when the door of the engineering office opened and a very happy Jack Evans walked in. He strode forward and grabbed my hand, shaking it almost violently.

"Hell," he said loudly, "never... never thought my saviour could, or would, be you - they never told me you were here - of course, how could they know? I'm told it was all down to you and that the little bastard in the front office was to blame by trying to disguise his incompetence. How can I thank you."

"Think nothing of it Jack," I said still shaking his hand and feeling unburdened from a fifteen-year-old sense of blame. "Here," I said, pressing a small yellow plastic duck into his hand, "a small memento of another time. Do you fancy a cup of coffee?"

Limited Options

I could have avoided a lot of trouble if only I had listened to the radio more intently. I was about to leave the house and was just getting my nursing outfit finalised and checking my clinical kit when the local news came on reporting the closure of the high street due to flooding from a burst water main.

The centre of town, said the announcer, was knee deep in water and the police had sealed off all approaches while the water company got to grips with the problem.

This was a damned nuisance because it meant I was being forced to bypass my normal route to work - assuming I could that is, with everyone else trying to do the same thing! As this sunk in, my mind began to ponder on the best option given the circumstances.

Had I waited to digest the radio report more fully I would have heard the announcer say that coincidentally, the southern access to the town was also inaccessible due to a house fire near the road. I only managed to register the initial part of the report so that remained fixed in my head as I cheerfully set off on foot.

I knew my town very well, but for every alternative route I chose I eventually hit a police barrier. At last, as I sneaked through a few narrow back alleys I eventually turned out on to the main southern access. However, as I did so I became instantly aware that I had made a fundamental mistake. A hundred meters ahead of me I saw large striped, red and white barriers that the police had slung across the whole road to block it. In the distance I could see scores of intermixed police and fire tenders and the sporadic appearance of flashing blue lights, all periodically smothered by billowing black smoke.

What should I do?

I pulled out my mobile, phoned the hospital, and almost immediately heard the switchboard pick up the call. It was Sandra, the communications supervisor.

"Sandra - this is Cathy Sanderson nursing sister on Tolman Ward, I'm going to be late, that is if I make it at all, I can't seem to get to the hospital by the usual routes - have you heard about it?"

She heard Sandra let out a "Huh" and "Tell me about it... hardly anyone south of the hospital has made it in... why do you think I'm manning the switchboard? If this goes on we are in one hell of a pickle - with so many being called in as absent from duty we're cancelling a lot of routine procedures and trying to cope with volunteers from the night staff and a skeleton medical support crew but it's going to be very tricky. Try and get in if you can Cathy - we need everyone we can get."

The last remark was said with a sense of panic and as I gave Sandra an 'I'll do all I can.', I realised how catastrophic the two events of fire and flood had become. Each incident was a crisis, but the two in combination represented a potential disaster for some very sick people.

If I wasn't able to solve this logistical problem, I was going to be very late for my duty shift - or not arrive at all. I considered all my options again. Could I find a back street route that would bypass both the flood and the fire? The more I thought about it the more I realised that no such route was possible.

In short, I was thwarted.

There was only one way I could think of, but as the idea formed, I instantly discarded it as potentially embarrassing. Yet, with no other way there was nothing for it. I worked at the hospital and needed to get there - and I needed to get there because the hospital needed me! So my strategy was clear.

If the situation prevented me from moving as an individual, they would have to let me through as an emergency.

Dialling an emergency on my mobile I asked for an ambulance to pick up a semi-conscience casualty from the fire, and gave the address as being where I currently was - that was, by the police barrier.

I lay down, banged myself gently on the head, and waited for my lift.

A Premium Moment.

The last week had been a nightmare. Artic weather, with unusually early snow sweeping in on strong winds, had made the equipment reluctant to start as diesel fuel had gelled in the tanks and frozen batteries had refused to turn over engines. Added to this predicament was a morass of tyre clogging mud and deep wheel ruts as temporary thaws came and went, and the constant logging churned up everything into a thick and sticky quagmire underfoot. It created excessive strain on all the multi-wheeled vehicles; all made worse as the logging trailers, already critically loaded, started to show stress fractures in the chassis'.

Zack Thomas fought the numbing cold which even through his thick, cold stiff, leather gloves made handling freezing metal tools a dangerous trial. As he wiped his gloves free of ice he mulled over his situation.

He'd been operating his logging business in the North American woodlands near the Canadian border for twenty years and he and his six man crew had seen more than their fair share of troubled times. He'd fought long and hard to get profitable supply contracts, typically requiring fixed amounts of lumber to be delivered to the sawmills on a daily basis. Nevertheless, it meant that unless he kept to a tight schedule, his income could easily fall well below his outgoings.

Though he had invested heavily in specialised logging machinery and haulage equipment - which meant he could operate with the minimum of manpower coupled to the maximum possible efficiency - yet, it all came at a price. His financial commitments allowing for very little latitude in the ten sixty-ton loads the sawmills demanded every day. He and his crew worked at an exhausting pace, felling trees, removing all outgrowth besides the trunk, separating the hardwood from the softwoods, dividing trunks, loading the massive haulage trailers and preparing the next batch for shipment as one trailer left and another arrived back.

Now, with the numbing cold making the handling of machinery and tools a nightmare, he began to think that it simply wasn't worth it.

Zack and his team had already welded together two major faults in the frame of one logging trailer, and were about to attend to a wheel bearing fault on a tree cutter, when a four by four truck nosed it's way into the clearing through glutinous mud.

"Hell - it's the insurance inspector." Zack heard one of his team spit out.

He turned to see Kevin Anderson, site inspector for Zenith Assurance, making an unsteady trudge from his truck.

"Damned conditions...wonder you don't call it quits when it's like this." Anderson called out.

Zack dropped the wrench he was holding and stood to meet Anderson as he approached.

"With the premiums I'm having to pay your firm you should be asking why I don't fit floodlights and work all through the night." he said.

Anderson smiled, it was the usual response and he expected nothing else from Zack Thomas. At $150,000 a year, Zack's insurance premium, given the nature of his business, was no laughing matter. He was obliged to cover a massive public liability, forest fire, accidental employee fatality, third party and irreparable machinery cover; it was - not to understate it - very expensive. The potential damages and compensation likely to be incurred if, for example, Zack's operations caused a forest fire were dire. As such, he had limited options regarding insurance and very few companies were prepared to offer any cover at all. Without it he was barred from working on publicly owned land. Zenith had reluctantly agreed, but only by setting an excessive premium and applying further conditions with periodic safety inspections. It was imposed to ensure it negated any risk of a major payout by Zenith.

"Wheredya wanna start?" Zack said shaking hands with Anderson.

Anderson smiled as he replied, "Anywhere where the mud doesn't suck my boots off! I'd kill for a coffee."

It was the usual routine with Anderson, and Zack made the usual reply.

"Yeah - I'll get a flask - wanna check the trailer first? We've just had to do some running repairs."

Zack turned and made for his own truck while Anderson headed back down the clearing to where the second haulage trailer was being loaded. As he approached, he ran his eye over the whole rig, somewhat surprised and rather impressed by the fact that all the tires, though mud caked, had no signs of severe attrition and likewise the motor cab and chassis. The youngest of the field crew showed him the frame repairs. The welding was professionally carried out and seemed more than adequate - a miracle given the conditions.

As he completed his survey of the rig Anderson heard Zack approach and turned to see him grimly holding two steaming mugs of coffee, intent on conserving the contents as the thick mud underfoot conspired to drag him down.

Anderson, too, glued down with the mud, lurched forward to meet Zack and relieved him of one mug just as it started to slop.

"The mud's less heavy over there if you want a break." Zack said, motioning towards a higher part of the clearing, "Let's make for it." As he turned he shouted at his crew "Get some coffee - warm up - thirty minutes!"

Zack had his pick-up parked on the higher ground and they eventually found themselves sitting in the pick-up's cabin with the engine running and the heater blowing warm air on to their near frozen bodies.

"Tough going in these conditions Zack - I don't envy you." Anderson's tone was genuine and sympathetic. Zack and he had a long personal history, and it was sheer coincidence that had him working for Zenith Assurance after an accident had broken him as a logger. Zack in turn appreciated that Kevin Anderson was a decent man - he was an expert woodsman and knew what it was like to work and survive in the current conditions.

"I guess it wouldn't be so bad if you had less to worry about in terms of debt... but as it stands you're on a financial tightrope and you can't afford a slip. Could you get the sawmills to offer better rates Zack?"

Zack sipped his coffee, asking himself the self-same question, as he had hundreds of times before, and knowing full well what the answer was.

"They won't offer more than they do, claiming that on price we hardly compete with imported woods - seems they can ship it in all the way from South America and still virtually undercut us. I'm not sure if it's completely true, but true enough for the mills to turn us away if they want to, and in these conditions we can hardly make the tonnage. In short, we're over a barrel! What would make a difference is if your outfit dropped their premium rate. This god-awful insurance is costing me nearly two thirds of my yearly outgoings."

Anderson grunted agreement. "You know, I've had another look at the small print in your policy. There are so

154

many caveats, exclusions and conditions that it's highly unlikely that Zenith would ever be liable. And, let's face it, I'm here; what I mean is that I'm being paid by Zenith to close the door on any possible claim you might make in those very few areas where they are liable. In effect, what limited liability they do have is virtually reduced to zero."

Zack took another sip of his rapidly cooling coffee. "Tell me about it - you're saying that like all insurance companies Zenith aim to reduce their risk, and thus their liability, to zero, yet all the time being able to suck in their exorbitant premium."

"That's it," Anderson nodded, "though I shouldn't say it of my employers...if I'm here to protect their interests it's because you are paying them a hefty premium and they are paying my fees out of your premium and cheerfully pocketing the rest. It's pure profit - little chance of loss; they know the risk of a legitimate claim from you is negligible."

Zack sank back in his seat and allowed the airflow from the heater to find the coldest part of his thighs. "So, if that is true, my insurance cover has no real value other than to gain official approval to work in the forest. Insofar as a claim is concerned, even if I made one, I hardly stand a chance."

Anderson offered a curt acknowledgement. "Yeah - it's Zenith's win, win approach - I guess you aren't alone."

Zack stayed silent as he heard the second haulage trailer arriving and the repaired unit coughing as it started up. His crew were a good team and he wanted to do the best for them and himself. He turned to Anderson. "Kevin, what is the minimum documentation I need to satisfy the logging license bureau?"

Anderson paused as he went over the application procedure in his mind. "Your business credentials, IRS tax, registration of company directors and so on, financial references from your bank, two character references, certified equipment to be used in the forest, supply contracts, notification to emergency services - and of course fire and public liability insurance."

As Zack re-absorbed the familiar list he made up his mind; but first he had to explore one other alternative.

"What does it take to actually insure someone against mishaps Kevin - look, I'm paying Zenith $150,000 a year for insurance they could wriggle out of, and ordinarily I couldn't fight them in the courts if they refused a claim without some pretty hefty resource behind me. But... say I gave you my next two years premium - you would be sitting on a substantial amount of money. Could you then set up an insurance operation with me as your only client?"

Anderson was forced to smile again, it was a good idea but he knew it wouldn't work.

"Sorry Zack, but it isn't that easy. First off - and the easiest part - you have to have financial reserves that on paper at least exceed your maximum potential liability. It would need close to - what - ten million and then some."

Zack sat silent for a moment and then, putting his empty mug onto the dashboard, opened the cab door and stepped down onto the rapidly freezing earth. As he closed the door he said, "Stay and keep warm Kevin - I just need to do something."

It was five minutes later when Kevin Anderson heard two ear-shattering reports, akin to an express train ploughing in to buffers at high speed. Turning to look through the windscreen he was shaken as he saw both of the snow laden haulage units with their trailer frames collapsed. Each appeared to have broken it's back; recently cut trunks were scattered left and right where the side props had been torn away.

A small gaggle of men, enveloped in clouds of condensation from their hot breath, appeared from behind the massive bulk of the loading crane and moved forward to survey the wreckage. One, obviously Zack Thomas, broke away from the others and made his way laboriously towards the pickup, his hunched body struggling through the slowly congealing mud and driving snow. After a short time, he reached the pickup, opened the door and lifted himself into the drivers seat. He said nothing as he slammed the door shut, blowing a small gust of snowflakes and cracked icicles towards Anderson. Instead, he reached for his flask and on retrieving his mug from the dashboard top, poured in more coffee.

"Want some Kevin?" he asked, a curious twinkle in his eye.

Entirely bemused, Anderson meekly held out his mug and as Zack tilted the flask, watched the steaming coffee start to fill his mug.

"Did I see what I thought I saw? Anderson asked.

Zack nodded, "You saw both my haulage units break their backs as we loaded them - too cold, see! The load levels are lower if the steel is frozen - but you didn't know that did you Kevin?"

He damned well did, but said nothing.

"Thing is Kevin, I'm going to have to shut down now...can't operate without the haulage units. It means too that I am going to put in a claim to Zenith for two new trailers and financial compensation for loss of business. Now as I recall, a claim has to be put in within 24 hours of an incident... yes?"

Anderson dipped his head sharply in confirmation.

"Well, accept this as an official notification of a claim Kevin - we'll do all the paperwork, but given the conditions I doubt you will be able to submit it in time. That means Zenith will refuse it - but hell, they would anyway! That means I would have to sue them for an unreasonable decision if I could afford it. But, don't you see - now I can! I can't work anymore, so I won't need the insurance that, as you know, has its premium due next month. It means Zenith will also know I have $150,000 to pay my lawyers and litigate at any level Zenith likes. Zenith won't fight; it will cost them too much financially and, more importantly, publicly. Think of all the business they'll lose if existing and potential customers learn that Zenith are out and out sharks. So all I have to do is frighten them for long enough to get them to the negotiating table."

Anderson listened with ever rising admiration, "And then, what Zack? What are you after?"

Zack grinned triumphantly "I'll insist Zenith offer me reasonable terms as regards cover - I'll accept your inspections so you will not lose your job. But Zenith will remove all the small print on the policy at a very much-reduced yearly premium. With the extra money I can expand my operations and output more lumber to the sawmills. For me it will be a win-win outcome."

Kevin Anderson could hardly believe his ears - but his friend was right. Zenith had effectively shot themselves in the foot by being so calculating and greedy. Had they been more reasonable then Zack would have neither the reason, nor the resource, to embarrass them. Now they were in for a shock. Unless of course something totally unexpected happened - that regardless of how long the claim was delayed, Zenith actually agreed to pay it!

Music To My Ears

As I closed the door of the apartment behind me, I heard the mournful sound of the bells and strings that preceded the saddest aria from Puccini's *Tosca*. I should have anticipated it, my flatmate Benjamin Elgar was home.

I suppose that having a name like Elgar should have made his love of classical music and opera a foregone conclusion, but his almost pathological liking for deeply passionate and emotionally fraught melodies, at any time of day or night, was not easy to live with. To often the music I heard from his expensive Hi-Fi system was sullen and brooding and to be honest, to me very depressing.

"Ben - want some tea?" I shouted, trying to penetrate the ever-rising crescendo from the tenor and his manic accomplices in the orchestra. Ben twisted in his padded chair, currently orientated toward his gigantic loudspeakers, and smiled his typical happy smile. And there was the rub; whatever his taste in music Ben was the happiest of souls - no amount of sad, tortured melodies could dampen his irrepressible and exuberant disposition. That, I suppose, was the one great consolation about his tastes in music - and the fact that it didn't last forever.

Eventually he had the good sense to realise that his preferences were a personal thing, and so he never imposed it on me for any extended length of time. A few minutes later I heard the final bars of Tosca drain away into silence followed by a slight pop from the speakers as Ben switched the system off.

"Tea - oh lovely." he said as I poured two mugs full of brew and handed him his.

"Good day?" I asked as I searched for a biscuit in the ever-empty biscuit barrel.

"Not bad - got a request for a very obscure title this p.m., a rare variation on a Cossack folk song updated by Rachmaninoff in 1902. Took me well over three hours to identify it and track down a copy." Ben beamed a smile of satisfaction that I suppose was natural. He worked in the rare scores and musical manuscripts section at the British Library and to him it was paradise and heaven rolled in to one.

Did he have the job because of his remote relationship to the famous British composer? Well yes - but also because his knowledge of music over the ages was second to none and he was rarely found wanting.

"Mind if I borrow your music system over the next few days?" I asked, "I'm composing a brief for a libel case and I think I might do it in the peace and quite here rather than in the office. A little music in the background could be relaxing - and of course stimulating."

Ben smiled an acknowledgement, which as usual bespoke a curious puzzlement as to how it was that a musical genius and a lawyer could ever become such close friends.

"Sure - just don't blow out the speakers - I know you."

He was right of course, our tastes were diametrically opposite, I had a liking for fifties bubble gum music which included Doo-Wop and driving Rock and Roll; which to Ben appeared not so much anathema, more a logical distortion of the term music, to him it was akin to naming a five foot rowing dinghy 'Titanic'. Still, on the face of it he was not only tolerant of my peculiar musical preferences, but never made the effort to criticise or deprecate what I liked.

Over the next few days I was the one who was there in the apartment when Ben came in from work. He was hardly timely in his arrival - 4.00pm one day, 5.30pm the next. Ben periodically wandered away early from his daily duties at the BL, especially when he was immersed in his antiquarian pursuits and needed to do some research elsewhere. It was inevitable that quite often he would arrive back at the flat with some of my music blaring away. At first he simply withdrew and dived into a book or two but as the weekend wound on into Monday he began to absent himself from the flat for long periods. I was too busy to bother myself with his reasons why, and just got on with what I was doing.

After a couple of days I realised that I had taken on a lot more in terms of the brief than I had expected, and it was going to take much longer than I thought. I certainly wasn't going to be able to undertake my bi-weekly cooking roster for the two of us.

"Ben, I'm going to need some more time here and I'm afraid and it's going to have to be nose to the grindstone - can you fend for yourself for a while longer - I mean, I'll eat out, you try to eat at the BL canteen," Ben looked at me with less than a grateful stare but quietly acquiesced.

It was the middle of the next Friday afternoon that I finally completed all of the brief and decided to relax by listening to some more of my favourite Rock n' Roll. As the first opening bars of Eddie Cochran's *'Summertime Blues'* came up I gave the amplifier volume control a twist forward and sat down to get deafened by the sound.

I had my eyes closed as the CD rolled through its titles. I was full of anticipation as Buddy Holly's *'Peggy Sue'* was about to be superseded by Little Richard's *'Long Tall Sally'* when the sound was cut off instantly.

I came out of my reverie and opened my eyes to see Ben standing by the hi-fi stack looking intently at me. What I saw in his glistening, unblinking eyes sent a shiver down my spine.

"What the hell Ben - what's wrong, why did you kill it, was it too loud?" He shrank down, his head dropping forward into a cowed stance.

"I can't stand it - my work, it's gone to hell. I can't think - I..."

"I rose to my feet and went over to him. He looked bad - as I had never seen him - haggard and downcast.

"Are you ill - shall I call a doctor?" I asked.

He shook himself away from me.

"No - not a doctor. It's just that bloody cacophony you call music. Please... don't you know... every day and night for the last eight I've been here, or come in, and I'm exposed to what you are playing. I don't know if I can stand it anymore - it's... it's just too overpowering, too exciting, too damn infectious. It's depressing me! I'm tapping my foot at work, remembering some of the rifts and harmonies and... well, it stops me thinking straight. I can't concentrate and I'm making mistakes like a novice. You don't understand do you - I can only function at one level, anything that interferes with my internal musical identity confuses me. Your music is like a knife slicing out parts of my security - what I listen to, what I like, reinforces it, what you like disrupts it."

I watched as tears welled up in his eyes, it was shame, coupled with an abiding sorrow that he had so disappointed me.

I had no choice, I pressed the eject button on the CD player and replaced the CD in its case. It would be a long time before I heard these tracks again.

Now when I get home I know I'll find my old happy friend Ben again - even though I have to endure the misery that emanates from the speakers.

After all, his music affects me a damn sight less than my music affects him.

The Jokes On Me

I suppose the way I died was as near perfection as anyone might wish. My two well-lubricated friends and I were in the middle of a very friendly winters evening in our local village pub. We had swallowed yet another warming scotch and pep, and were about to defy the snow outside with even more amber liquid, when the less intoxicated of my two pals started telling us a joke.

I remember how we two attentive listeners, merry and warm by the blazing fire in the saloon, waited with glee as the joke slowly built to its hilarious punch- line. We hardly noticed the landlord as he came up to us with a tray carrying our next round of drinks, and he could only spare us a grunt as he saw how completely drawn in we were by our friends dramatic discourse. I was holding my thimble of scotch in my hand, sipping it eagerly, as the joke climaxed to the punch-line. It was more than hilarious, it was devastating. The joke climaxed not with one hysterically funny punch-line, but two - the second so outrageous that as I struggled to put down my glass to avoid spilling it, my heart stopped!

You might say I was lucky. The pub was full of regulars and our local GP was one of them. They tell me he got to me pretty fast and applied resuscitation - long enough for the newly arrived paramedics to hook me into a defibrillator and re-start my heart. Someone later told me that they remarked I was the happiest looking corpse they had ever seen!

I was in hospital for well over a fortnight as the surgeons key-holed their way into my chest and cleared out a few gummed up cardiac arteries. My ensuing convalescence

164

was a life style revolution - and became a boring routine of long walks, fresh fruit and constant nagging from my 'nearest and dearest' to refrain 'from doing what I had done before'!

But, it was strange! The caution was rather pointless, I had very little recollection of 'what I had done before', and particularly the night I had my heart attack, though I did recall fragments of the earlier part of the festivities. The rest, sadly, was (as memories go) a virtual non-event. And yet, I had a feeling there was something I wanted to remember - something that promised only good.

My two drinking chums politely refrained from detailing anything to do with the night in question - the momentous episode was treated as a bereavement, and not spoken of again. Since I had nothing in my memory to prompt them to tell me what I wanted to know, I was reluctant to embarrass them (and myself) by asking for details about something I knew they wanted to forget.

Time passed, and I suppose you could say that much of my curiosity regarding the night in question faded as my health and circumstances stabilised and became the 'status quo'. True, much could be credited to my improved lifestyle and renewed vigour for life. I only occasionally found myself in the pub and certainly not with my two drinking companions and a grumpy landlord - neither of whom wanted to see me keel over again. However, after one particularly long walk on a hot spring morning, I found myself rather dry and, passing the old tavern, I convinced myself that a half pint of ale would do me no harm; if it was limited to a half pint that was.

I was met with a smile from the barmaid and as she took my money I was able to view the inside of the saloon and the two other bars through an archway on the opposite side of the saloon. To my surprise, the laughter I heard was coming from three men propping up the opposite bar, and one of them was one half of my two erstwhile drinking companions. It was as fragments of the conversation drifted across to me that I realised I had heard some of it before, that is, it was a familiar theme. As I continued to listen, I was taken back to a particularly unpleasant experience - what I was hearing, so I thought, was 'the joke'.

The joke I could hear being recounted in the opposite bar was the one that precipitated for me at least a longish, death defying, stay in hospital. So there it was, a chance to face my nemesis - I had to know more!

I took my glass, and myself, around to the end of the public bar and gently pushed open the connecting door between the two bars. Now I could hear the voice relating the story very distinctly, and a good measure of forgotten memories came rushing back to me.

I listened for a while and began to get impatient as the long scene setting for the joke continued. The run-up wasn't precisely as my faulty recall would have it, but the story started to came together and with the voice droning on, I listened with a combination of foreboding and urgency, wanting the punch-lines to arise.

As I listened it all started to re-appear in my mind - the lead up to the first punch-line now echoed in my head and when it was at last voiced, it was accompanied by screams of disbelief. As the second punch line was spluttered out, with the originator hardly able contain himself, it was followed by a chorus of hysterical laughter which had them all in tears. I clutched my chest but somehow my trepidation was wasted. Oh yes, it was a very funny joke and deserved all the applause it got. But I had no need to worry, it was one of those jokes that seem to be funnier when your blood alcohol levels are about fifty fifty. I'm sure that it was concocted by some wit who was insightful enough to know what was funny when you were tipsy, and what wasn't.

As for me, I was not only stone cold sober but rather unimpressed - after all, I'd heard it all before!

Letter To An Only Child

I suppose I always thought, or used to think, that who I was, what I did, and the way I did it, was unique.

You shouldn't be surprised by this revelation, I'm an only child and we single offspring invariably believe that the world revolves around us rather than the other way around.

As I grew up my splendid isolation was never threatened by bitter experience or life's vagaries - I somehow managed to slip past any doubts or damage to my aloof and unyielding attitude. Indeed, I clung warmly to the old saying that *'you should never worry about an only child, the idea of failure never occurs to them'* as absolute proof of my identity. I breezed along through my teens and early twenties with failure desperately and hopelessly trying to catch up.

And true it was until I come across Samuel, who, like me, was a newly installed member of our law firm. You see, unbeknown to me Samuel was an only child too, and when he was installed in the office next to mine something almost supernatural took place.

Each morning we would grunt a greeting, but that was as far as it got. Somehow, we were instinctively, and mutually, suspicious and the tension between us hung like a grey cloud over the whole firm. We knew that we were in competition for the next upgrade within the firm, and there was no doubt that for every client's brief completed successfully we were at pains to ensure the senior partners knew about it.

That's not to say that I thought Samuel a sycophantic back stabber - that he never was. He conveyed a kind of dignity and pride as he busied himself in the outer offices and every now and again I felt a slight twinge of envy. But that was as far as it went - as far as I was concerned, he was an obstacle to my promotion and better lifestyle.

We were both well over a year into our junior partnerships when one of the senior partners instructed us to work together on a particularly troublesome brief. A woman was suing the police for wrongful arrest and mistreatment and she was insisting on an action for damages. The police, naturally, refuted the claim and so Samuel and I started to prepare all the material for a court hearing. I was out of the office on the day we were due to meet the client for further evidence and, arriving back a little late, it was clear that I had missed the boat. Samuel and an absolutely stunning woman were in conference and it was obvious that they were getting on well - too well my jealous heart told me, and that, I determined, would not do.

I walked in on a high spirited discussion and even though Samuel introduced me with all appropriate professional courtesy, the lady hardly gave me a glance. Her eyes were locked on to Samuel's and it was as if they had been lovers for ever. My spirits plummeted - Oh God, it was love at first sight!

Samuel was smitten - he had to be given the amount of work he did on the case. Burning the midnight oil was an understatement - he must have been drinking the stuff!

I kept my envy in check though I was well aware that the senior partners would not be at all happy if they found out that Samuel was having an affair with a client. Such liaison's were taboo. Still, my pride, and a sense of fair play, kept my mouth shut even though I drooled every time I saw her arrive for another 'interview'.

It was a few days after we had concluded the brief preparation and had sent it to counsel that we agreed that we had formulated a winning case against the police. We felt that we should now inform the client prior to counsel's opinion and Samuel gleefully arranged another visit by the lovely client.

Reluctantly I made myself scarce at the appointed time and was on my way down the dividing corridor to my office when the lovely lady in question came towards me.

"Hello - can you tell me where Samuel Cantwell's office is please?"

This was a strange query - she knew very well where Samuel's office was - golly, she even knew where his underwear was.

"Just down the corridor, as you know." I replied pointing at the door.

"Of course - it's a big building - lots of similar corridors!"

For a moment, I saw something new - dilated irises accompanied by a genuine 'I think you are nice' smile.

This threw me - wasn't she supposed to be enamoured with Samuel?

"Sure you can find it - shall I show you?" I mumbled, not sure if I read the signs right.

"I would appreciate it." she said and smiled again.

I turned to her side, inviting her to walk on, wondering what I had done to deserve this opportunity.

I knocked on Samuel's door and opened it to allow her in.

Again, the lovely smile "Shall I see you again?" she whispered.

169

I made a seemingly reckless reply, seeing that here might be a chance to take some of the shine off Samuel's conquest.

"My office is next door." I said, indicating with my arm.

I had left her for about thirty minutes when there was a faint rap on my office door.

"Come in." I croaked hoping it was her. And so it was.

She stood there with Samuel who, uncharacteristically for him, had escorted her to my office, reciprocating my earlier courtesy to him.

She and Samuel stood in the doorway. He held back and let her through and as she passed she said "Just a few words of thanks."

As she turned away from Samuel and he slowly closed the door I noticed that not once had I seen the same adoration in her eyes for Samuel that I had seen so many times before. Instead she seemed intent on me.

Was I upset?

No way!

Not to labour the point, we had an instant rapport. I don't even remember mentioning the fact that we were representing her in some rather serious litigation. Instead, we managed to detail our backgrounds and lives, likes and dislikes, favourite foods and everything that made us what we were. As noon approached, I suggested lunch and eventually two very happy people found themselves demolishing sandwiches and beer in a local bar.

"So your Samuel's right arm?" she queried as the last of her ham sandwich disappeared.

"Not at all!" I mumbled over a mouthful of egg mayonnaise,

"We just happen to have been paired on your case - usually we're working separately."

"Do you get much time together - I mean, compare notes and cases, talk about clients?"

This question was a little intrusive I had to admit, but I had no real reason to doubt its innocence.

"Seldom - in general lawyers are an introspective bunch and we like to keep our case notes and legal interpretation to ourselves until we have formulated the best approach we can. Furthermore, client confidentiality is paramount unless the case is subject to a team effort like yours. Even so, nothing private or personal gets discussed. As to my being Samuel's right arm, he has no need of me, nor me him."

When I left her it was with the promise of dinner the next evening and I had to admit it was a very pleasant thought - she was not only physically attractive but bright and charming - in a word irresistible. I mentally rubbed my hands thinking of Samuel's sorrow and displeasure when he found out that his amour had forsaken him. I took no notice of the fact that I too was now immersed in something unethical, and that I depended on Samuel being as discreet as I had been. On the way back to my office, I had no recollection of getting there - my glee and sense of joy overtook everything.

I spent the next day wishing the time away, willing the hands of the clock to go faster. As late afternoon dragged on I returned to my office with the umpteenth cup of coffee, the getting of which had become a ritual to occupy my time given that my case notes had become so boring that they might as well have been in a foreign language. It was as I sat in my chair, watching the wall clock tick on, that I heard a knock on the door. Before I could say anything the handle was turned and the door opened. Samuel appeared, his face and the piece of paper he held, heralding something ominous.

"Problem?" I said, waiting for an explanation.

He strode over to my desk and handed me the sheet of paper he was holding.

I read it, and read it again and as I did so a cold hand gripped my larynx and shook out a strangled groan.

The typewritten note said:

'Samuel - I want the £5000 within 48 hours, or I complain to your senior partners that you coerced a client into having sex with you. Remember, I can verify everything I will be disclosing. Also - whatever else I decide to do, you will not interfere.'

I knew the signature, I had seen it many times on the papers dealing with her case notes. My heart dropped into my stomach, and it was all I could do not to wail or weep. Somehow I held back my crushed soul.

"What now." I managed to croak not knowing where to look.

"Nothing, he said, "she's under arrest, I had no option but to report it. I had you and her followed by a private eye and had her background checked. Seems she was very good at subtle - and not so subtle - forms of blackmail. We should have looked more closely at the police arrest forms. Until the CPS dropped the case they were intending to charge her with extortion. For extortion read blackmail. I'm sorry - it hurts doesn't it?"

I looked at Samuel, and he at me.

I'm damn sure that at that moment we two realised that we were as gullible and as human as the rest of the crowd. We had been taught a lesson - a bitter lesson - that we weren't particularly special or unique. As to being superior - no way - we were as vulnerable, and on the same level, as the next person.

I watched Samuel, no doubt with a pleading look, hoping for solace, but an ironic smile began to develop across his face. We both started to laugh at what was an unspoken, but mutual revelation, that we saw in each other the same arrogant fool.

We had both experienced a salutary lesson that was long overdue - now, years on, and both of us senior partners, I still shudder when I think of how close we both were to disaster. I detect a certain humility in Samuel now, and no doubt he sees the same in me.

As we gained influence in the firm we introduced one further rule - all lone female clients were to be chaperoned during an interview - after all, some of our male junior partners may not realise that they are no more than children.

Facing A Counterfeit

I had been up and down the High Street twice hoping to find a hardware shop that sold the adhesive I wanted. It was a clammy, cold and bone numbing December day and the wind chill factor was starting to bite through my top coat and into my spirits.

I had passed the local coffee shop twice in my travels and as I returned down the High Street for the third pass, the smell of roasted coffee beans was too much of a temptation.

I found myself sat in a window seat, absorbing the warmth of the cafe and relishing the fresh Cappuccino resting on the tabletop in front of me. As I sipped from my cup, I was able to look out onto the pavement, watching as the huddled crowds hurried to get done whatever it was they needed to do and fly home to a warm house.

I was so engrossed in my own thoughts that I almost ignored the sudden appearance of a face that peered in at me and smiled through the frost edged glass to my right.

The man was clearly pleased to see me, but I failed to recognise the individual and was most definitely disinclined to smile back.

I waited with less than any interest as the stranger came in to the cafe and ordered a coffee at the counter. I excused his embarrassing behaviour as a case of mistaken identity on his part, and hoped he had by now seen the error of his ways.

I was completely taken aback then when he suddenly appeared to the side of my table.

"Hello John." he said, a huge smile on his face. As I looked up and scrutinised the face above me, I again was unable to place it.

"Do I know you?" I asked.

"Yes, I think you do - may I sit down?"

Reluctantly, I gestured in the direction of the empty seat opposite me.

Putting his coffee down on the tabletop, he sank into the seat and once again gave me a beaming smile.

"You think we are acquainted?" I asked as he shuffled in his seat to get comfortable. Again, he simply smiled.

"I sure you are mistaken," I added "I'm fairly good with names and faces and I'm certain we have never met."

"Perhaps not formally," he replied in a very warm voice "but we have met - I never forget a face and, in your case, a pair of eyes."

This remark lost me. Was he slightly unhinged, trying to be sarcastic or sincerely labouring under a delusion.

I was about to offer a gentle riposte when he said "My name is Richard Eddington."

For a moment I pondered on whether this name had any significance for me - but it didn't

"I'm sorry - I don't recognise you or your name." I answered.

"That's okay - I imagine you must see hundreds of people in your line of work and I can see how easily it would be for you not to remember most of them - I'm just one of your grateful successes."

"Explain please." I said though by now I was beginning to get a hint of what he was coming to.

"You're at St Elizabeth's Hospital aren't you?" he said, "Anaesthetist?"

Well, one thing was certain from his last remark - at that moment he knew more about me than I did of him.

"True." I said waiting for what, from that moment, I had almost instantly come to expect.

"I'm Richard Eddington." he repeated "Two years ago I was badly injured in a car crash and my face was so damaged that it was beyond salvaging. That night, you and the two senior reconstructive surgeons took me into the operating theatre and removed what was left of my face and grafted on the face of a young man who had died from his injuries three hours before. What you see is the result of your humanity and handiwork. I will ever be grateful for what you and your colleagues did - the more so since this face is ten years younger than the one I started with, and my life has become richer for it. I have a new job, a new wife and everything has turned out for the better. Seeing your eyes over your mask, as I lost consciousness from the anaesthetic, was the most reassuring thing I remember about that time - so I'm here to say how grateful I am."

I had to smile back at him - now I remembered that fateful night and the effort it took to get him the only treatment open to us. I only saw the new face from the wrong side of the operating table, so that limited my recollection of its features.

I was just about to compliment him on how well the graft had taken when a small gaggle of people burst in to the cafe and stared at us.

"See, see!" cried a well-dressed thirties something woman pointing and waving theatrically. "It is Michael, I told you I had seen him in the street."

176

Grinning with abject joy, she virtually ran to our little table towing four other obviously happy people behind her. She made no effort to halt her momentum and literally threw herself into the seat besides Richard Eddington. She looked hard at him as her motion suddenly stopped, and though he was aghast with surprise, he had no chance to stop her suddenly throwing her arms around him in an emotional embrace.

"Oh darling - darling Michael." she wept into his shoulder, "We couldn't believe it when we saw you - they told us you were dead!"

Peep Hole

We had always lived in the old manor house, father had inherited it as the ninth in a long line of baronets. It wasn't as big as some estate houses, and the original lands had shrunk to a few acres, as generations of the family had kept financially afloat by selling off the estate's land for re-development.

I grew up with my sister Anna and my younger brother Mark. Though I, Edward, was first in line of inheritance, at the age of ten I was blissfully unaware of the burdens yet to fall on me - though my fathers premature grey hair should have told me something. Even so, our childhood was a constant and delightful romp around the house and gardens, and even though I was unable to follow my father into a famous public school, I somehow managed to survive at the nearby grammar school. This antiquated institution pretended academic privilege and the lofty prestige of offering scholarships and taking in borders.

Our old manor house was a warren of dusty unused rooms that entertained my siblings and me with all the cobwebbed residue of the family's past extravagances and fashionable indulgences. The one thing that stands out in my memory was the array of paintings that lined the middle staircase adjacent to what had been originally the 'great hall' but to us had become the 'common room'. It was here that the family gathered after meals or when mother and father occasionally entertained.

As I grew up a little, I had noticed that one of the staircase paintings, a splendid Victorian depiction of my great grandfather, had a strange defect in the old man's eyes.

Curious to establish what it was I observed, I one day commandeered a small stepladder from the kitchen and, waiting for the family to migrate to the garden, I propped the step ladder precariously between two stairs and the staircase wall, and climbed up to inspect the painting.

To my surprise, the eyes were not part of the painting - well, not the same piece of canvas. Instead, they were painted on to a thin shutter which, as I ran my finger along it, slid back under the slightest of pressure! As it moved back, with me wobbling on my shaky ladder, I was presented with a view of the common room, but not as I knew it.

The fireplace, a beautifully carved granite and alabaster inglenook, was still there - but the décor and furniture were definitely unknown to me. If anything, my inexperienced eyes saw oldness - a recognition that these things were of a past age.

As I took in the scene I heard a noise and fearing I would be caught doing something I should not be doing, I closed the shutter and scrambled down the stepladder so quickly that I was very nearly forced to repeat some school gymnastics. As it was, I was back to the kitchen returning the ladder, and out again looking perfectly innocent, before I realised that there had been no need of haste. The family were still in the garden.

Over the months I found two more opportunities to peep into the eyes of my grandfather and each time the scene in the common room was different. First the furniture became heavy dark wood and the walls were oak panelled with heavy carvings and armour breastplates. The last time I climbed the ladder the fireplace was gone. All I could see were rushes on the floor and massively heavy smoke stained joists and timbers. Even the light was sullen and dim.

None of this frightened me - it simply left me puzzled. What was I seeing - what was it I had seen? My inclination was to ask my father, but if I had he would want to know how I had accessed the painting. It was too risky - far riskier than climbing the stepladder. I decided to leave the subject for a while, but perhaps my musings and change of behaviour had been noticed, as one day my father took me into his study.

"Eddy" (he always called me Eddy, never Edward) "Is school okay? Are you having any problems?"

I shook my head but declined to answer.

"Well, something's wrong - you are not yourself. Can't you tell me?"

"Nothing is wrong father - it's just-"

"Just what - come on boy, a problem shared and all that. Can't we work it out together? Two heads are better than one."

As I related my story, very haltingly, watching my father's reaction as I told him about climbing up to the painting, I was relieved to see a hint of a smile appear on his face. The smile broadened as I recounted my observations looking through the painting's eye slit.

As I concluded, he remained silent for a minute. Then he gave me a slight hug.

"Well Eddy, now you know - well some of it. You beat me to it - I was sixteen before I tried to see what you have seen but I went a little further. Come with me."

He led me into the common room and turned me to face the opposite side of the staircase wall. He pointed upward but I could see nothing of interest until my eyes noticed a blemish in the light blue embossed wallpaper.

He told me to remain where I was and after a few minutes returned carrying a folding stepladder from the garden tool-shed. He leant the ladder against the wall - just below the blemish, and told me to climb up while he steadied the ladder from below.

I knew what was expected of me and as I reached the blemish, I saw it was the same shape as the slit in the painting. I looked down at my father for an unspoken permission to slide it back, and he gestured his agreement.

The piece of embossed paper slid as easily as had the one on the other side - or so it seemed. But what I expected to see was not here - the staircase within view was the one I knew, but now illuminated with brilliant sunlight from a vast transparent dome which overhung the old entrance hall and the opposite picture gallery. The pictures were the same but now seemed to be encased in transparent plastic mouldings. Likewise, looking down, the door to the old servants corridors was distinctly unusual - it was shimmering, as though it was less than solid, and was overhung with a sign that said 'No Access For Visitors'.

I was aghast and dumbly closed the slit and began to descend the ladder.

"No, no boy - open it again." I heard the order from my father.

I looked down and he was gesturing for me to re-climb the ladder. I obeyed immediately

The slit opened noiselessly and smoothly, and this time I was completely dumbfounded. This time the staircase was still in evidence but by virtue of the obvious differences in it's shape had clearly been re-constructed. The brilliant light from the dome had gone - replaced by what appeared to be a complete field of artificial light radiating from a source above the staircase illuminating a replica of the entrance hall. This was now formed of a lustrous wood coloured, material, seemingly continuous and framing the two outer main doors each of which shone with it's own glow of soft radiation. Opposite, the panelling still boasted the plastic encased paintings but there were fewer than before. The shimmering door to the servants quarter had gone - replaced with what appeared to be a person-sized booth made of some semi-transparent material. I was intent on this when suddenly the whole thing shivered and scintillated, and a body suddenly materialised inside the booth. I stared in disbelief, watching a somewhat familiar person walk away from the booth in absolute silence and disappear from my view.

The more I looked the more I recognised the features of the man. It made no difference that his clothing was a well fitted one piece suit, that it caught the light and reflected it like a rainbow. It was the face which was unforgettable - he looked just like me!

I pulled the slit shut and climbed down the steps like someone in shock - and even at my tender years that was how I felt. As I stood on *terra firma* and faced my father, he smiled a smile of sympathy and waited patiently for me to say something. I found it impossible - I was speechless and unable to comprehend what I had seen. What my eyes had told me my brain was still unable to register.

It was as I felt the flood of emotion overtake me, and tears well up in my eyes, that my father spoke.

"It's okay Eddy - it's a worm hole, a break in the fabric of space and time. It allows a glimpse of the past in one direction, a glimpse of the future in another. It's not dangerous and has only one real use it -"

"But father - I saw me - I saw myself - I'm sure I did but I was dressed in a dazzling suit, I was..."

"Sure - I saw me too didn't I - but was it me? Remember the background - the future state of things. How could you still be there so many years into the future? That wasn't you but it was your flesh and blood - our descendent, many generations hence.

It was then that I saw the reason my father had confidence in the future, regardless of what problems beset us now. He already knew that the old house would remain in the family no matter what.

After all, our descendents had shown us - they were just next-door!

Fool's Paradise?

"It's too early." I heard Monica say, "My eyes are hardly focusing."

The five o'clock start to get the newspapers sorted in our small village newsagents, particularly on a cold, wet Monday morning, was always a supreme effort. At least on a Sunday Monica and I could get an extra forty-five minutes in bed before waiting for the delivery.

"Have another coffee." I said, attempting to be sympathetic but feeling hardly better myself. "I'll take the counter trade later and you can pop off to bed for a while."

She'd smiled appreciatively as another pile of the *Daily Express* was mixed in with the *Telegraph,* the *Daily Mail* and the *Daily Mirror* for the soon to arrive paper boys and girls who delivered in and around the village environs.

"Don't be silly." she said, "You need some help for the morning rush - I'll take a break later."

I expected no less, Monica was always one to pull her weight and I suppose that was one of the many reasons I loved and valued her so.

We had been together for so long I had almost forgotten how much I had grieved before I found the tape recording of us going through a typical Monday morning. Hearing her gentle voice though the loudspeaker gave her presence back to me, and every time I played the tape through our old reel to reel I could see her as if she was still with me.

Now, as always, we completed the piles of papers together, her in the past brought to life by the audio tape - me alone and working methodically; my soul held together by a voice I adored.

After I switched off the tape I would take a long coffee break and think of the sweet, passionate bond that Monica and I had shared. Fifty years had passed and yet we were as empathetic, and as loving, as when we had first met. My mind would wonder back over all our good and bad times, only to be torn from it's reminiscences by the chiming of the wall clock. Then, just before I opened the shop for the early business, I would dig into the depths of my heart and whisper to her how I missed her.

No one would ever know my morning routine - and why should anyone know? It was a private thing between Monica and myself. Later on, as the day was finished, I would go to the cemetery and tend her grave, knowing that even though she was gone, tomorrow she would speak to me.

Preoccupation

I suppose I must have been pre-occupied, so I entirely missed the arrival of my old friend Martin Gale.

I was in Mayfields, the towns largest department store trying to find a pair of trousers to fit my ever-expanding waistline. It was a sad fact that I'd had no good reason to try on my more formal wardrobe for over two years, so when the wedding invitation for Martin's impending marriage arrived, I dug out all my mothballed suites to select an appropriate one.

To my dismay neither of my choices would fit anymore, the waistbands being at least three inches too small.

Martin smiled at me as, a little embarrassed, I quickly and sheepishly returned three pairs of trousers to the display stand rail.

"Hello Ted." he said, "Not happy with any of those?"

Truth to tell I was, one of the selection matched a suit top of mine almost exactly but I was momentarily embarrassed by the risk of having to explain why I needed it. His discovering that would have had them laughing for weeks down at our local watering hole.

"Maybe Martin," I replied, there's a lot to chose from - by the way, how are the wedding plans going? Everything on course?"

He nodded and smiled. "So far, but a few snags to iron out. But we'll get there."

I told him how I was looking forward to seeing him and his new (well, second hand) bride, and commented on the difficulty of getting arrangement of shirt, tie, suit and foot-ware for the wedding.

He gave a knowing look and came closer as if to confide in me.

"Truth is Ted, I'm beginning to wish it wasn't all necessary - I've got four suits and would you believe it, not one of the bloody things fits me anymore. I suppose I shouldn't be surprised, I haven't worn one for six years - at your wedding in fact."

A sudden thought flashed into my mind.

"Martin you used to be a lot bigger than me - when you say your suits don't fit, do you mean they are too big for you now?"

He made a gesture of agreement. "Too true - like a sack around a bean pole."

It was what I wanted to hear. "I've put on a lot of weight Martin I need a thirty six waist - you?"

"Now? Well a thirty three is ideal."

The wedding was one to remember - beautiful weather, an ecstatic wedding party and everyone calling me Martin until they saw my face. Martin was a 'Ted' for a short while and almost signed the register that way.

My only regret was that I never actually liked Martin's choice of suits - nor he mine, but beggars can't be choosers! Years later, when on occasion I recounted the story to various friends and family members, I never failed to emphasis the fact that my state of mind on the day I had encountered Martin in the department store was one of pre-occupation. Never for one moment thinking that the suits we were each to wear at the wedding, had also been - pre-occupied!

Unexpected Consequences

The car in front was going way too fast - 110 miles per hour and definitively increasing its speed as the dual carriageway emptied of other vehicles. It was a damned nuisance, he was on his way to the police station to clock off from his duty shift and now he had a maniac in an Aston Martin ignoring his siren and blue lights and forcing him to overtake.

He dropped a gear and forced the accelerator pedal down as far as it would go, hoping to heaven that the last service on his police *Subaru Impreza* had been carried out meticulously. All he needed was a spontaneous failure at these speeds and his family would be burying him.

He felt the surge of power come in.

Drifting to the outer lane, he began to overtake the Aston at a dangerous 130 mph.

As he did so he realised that even driving a powerful interceptor like the *Suburu*, he didn't have anything like the Aston's power, and the driver of the V12 *Aston Martin Vantage* could still easily pull away up to 190 mph without even trying. To his relief, the Aston started to drop away behind him and very gradually he brought himself and the Aston to a stop on the hard shoulder.

As he rolled to a stop, he called in his position and the Aston's registration number and exited the car as the driver of the Aston came walking towards him.

"Good evening officer, I'm…."

"Sorry? I should think so sir… I am too. I don't like having to exceed 130 mph for any reason, let alone for an idiot like you. The speed limit along here is 70 mph - you were clocking over 120."

The man scowled and looked down at his shoes. He was dressed rather scruffily, a pair of jeans, a rather careworn open necked shirt and black leather casual shoes showing tartan socks - apparently, not the typical well dressed owner of a £130,000 Aston Martin Vantage.

"Is this your car sir?"

"Yes, I am Nigel Eldridge, you can check with DVLA if you wish - I am in a hurry constable. Can we get this matter completed please, you should be aware..."

Huh, he did not intend to complete anything until due process had been carried out. He was definitely going to be late home, and his wife's evening meal, and her patience, was forfeit. As such, the man in front of him was getting no concessions.

"First things first sir. Your car keys please!"

He always ensured that as he left irresponsible drivers he ensured they could not leave him in a cloud of dust as they drove off, thereby starting another dangerous pursuit. With obvious reluctance, the man handed over a heavy bunch of bright alloy keys.

He made no reply and turned to make his way back to the *Subaru*. Regardless of his potentially lost dinner, he made no effort to hasten, and spent some time taking down the DVLA particulars off the ANPR screen. Armed with what he needed, he sauntered back to the driver who, as he approached, was clearly agitated.

"Now look here constable, do you know who I am, I'm..."

He shrugged mentally. There was no time to listen to the usual 'I'm an arrogant big shot and you have neither the authority nor the class to continue this impertinent confrontation'.

He raised his voice above that of the driver.

"According to our records you are Nigel Eldridge sir, and I'm glad to say your particulars are in order. Now sir, I am required to ask you for a breath test, so if you will oblige me I want you to blow into this tube and keep blowing until I say stop. Do you understand?"

The man's face had turned crimson.

"Listen to me you officious little autocrat, I'm supposed to be at Martingales Hospital by now, and there will be…"

He stepped close to the angry driver with only inches between them.

"I don't care what you want sir, and if you abuse me verbally again I will be forced to add insulting behaviour to charges of excessive speed, dangerous driving, failing to stop and, if you continue like this, refusal to take a breath test."

The driver glared at him in total defiance.

"Damn you, I haven't refused anything and if you don't stop being so bloody self-important for a moment I will tell you why…."

It was all he was prepared to tolerate. He thrust the alcohol tester into his pocket and, grabbing the man by the shoulders, forced him around and forward, effectively frog marching him towards the Subaru.

With a gasp of astonishment, the driver attempted to twist away.

"You think you are inviolate don't you, you think you can treat me like this with impunity you jumped up little tyrant. I guarantee you that no matter what happens to me your Chief is going to make you wish you were in another job. You may well be responsible for more misery than you could ever…"

He'd heard it all before. My wife's about to give birth, I'm on the way to the hospital - my son, brother mother or father are dying, I have an urgent appointment with my dentist, lawyer, member of parliament or chiropodist. My wife's stranded at the bus station with our two children, the vet says our dog is very ill and needs to be put down, the council are going to evict us unless I get back to the house or, more often, I'm late for a funeral.

Oh yeah, he'd heard it all before and then some.

Nearly every excuse, every denial of responsibility, and every threat in the book, and never once followed through in any way. They always wailed and blustered but it meant nothing. This one might be wealthy, but just wait until he saw the summons from the Crown Prosecution Service - his expensive lawyers would dry his eyes and simply tell him to cough up and look pretty, and not to dare to think of any kind of retaliation.

But this one was different because the struggle was still ongoing - now on top of the *Subaru* bonnet - and he had only just got the handcuffs on when another patrol car pulled in behind a small gaggle of vehicles and stopped. He waited, only half listening to the protestations coming from the Aston's driver as two familiar faces exited their car and made towards him.

He let go of his prisoner as his two colleagues took over the detention.

"Tell the custody sergeant the charges include threatening and insulting behaviour towards a police officer, reckless driving, failing to deliver a breath test and supplementary offences. I will make out the witness statement tomorrow morning after I report first thing. Tell him I'm not returning to the car pool - I'll sort it out tomorrow. He's all yours. I've been off duty for the last twenty minutes and I have some diplomacy to practice with my wife. She's going to kill me!"

His two colleagues smiled sympathetically and ushered the furious looking driver towards their own car.

Again, the driver blurted out his dissent.

"You rat, you excuse for a human being. Believe me when I tell you that you haven't heard the last of this - if it's the last thing I ever do I will…"

191

The last he heard was a confused and baffled babble of invective as the prisoner was persuaded to take the back seat of the second police car and the door was slammed shut.

He grinned as the principle driver of the second police car gave a double thumbs-up at the prospect of driving the *Aston Martin* back to the police station He felt a slight twinge of regret that it wasn't him that would be at the wheel of the *Vantage*, but unfortunately other duties came first.

He drove fast, using the police car as a personal guarantee of not being stopped by a colleague. Strictly speaking, use of a patrol car as personal transport was a big 'no no', but given the circumstances, it was unlikely that he would face any disciplinary charges - it was a minor transgression. In any case, he would not be using it again until he was officially on duty in the morning, so unless he was reported by the car pool super' on suspicion of personal use, he was okay.

He squeezed the patrol car onto the house forecourt. He was thankful that his wife's car was not alongside his own and occupying all the remaining space, thereby forcing him to park the patrol car on the street.

Strangely, there were no lights on in the house, and as he let himself in with his key he sensed that something was amiss.

He called out, but was met with silence.

His wife Janet was obviously not at home and he was at a loss to know what to do next. Normally she would tell him in good time if she was going to be away; very seldom did she do anything spontaneously, or without finding a way to notify him of a change of routine.

With all the lights on in the house he could find nothing to indicate what had called her away. There was no note - no message of any kind and no sign that an evening meal had been prepared.

It would not do to panic or presume something ominous, he could imagine Janet chiding him for jumping to the wrong conclusions. He imagined he could hear her scolding laugh "-and you being a policeman too!"

He made some tea and a sandwich, switched on the TV to catch the end of the news and wondered if, regardless of what teasing he might get, he should be more concerned.

It was as he pondered on the next sensible thing to do, to check with Janet's girl friends by phone, that he heard the front door chimes.

He looked through the bay windows of the lounge and in the oncoming darkness he could see the sidelights of another police car parked on the street behind his own patrol car now stationary on the forecourt access.

A slight chill ran down his spine and he strode rapidly to the front door.

The two uniformed officers were unknown to him - they were City and he was County.

"Officer Clifford?"

"Yes"

"Bad news I'm afraid - your wife was involved in a hit and run outside the supermarket at Thameshampton this afternoon. Unfortunately, her bag and all her ID wasn't handed in until she had been taken to hospital - it took some time for the one to get associated with the other. You need to get to the neurological department of Martingales Hospital asap. If you are ready, we'll get you there."

He didn't hesitate and slammed the front door behind him as he nodded his assent.

The city boys used their sirens and left rubber on the tarmac as they ate up the miles and soon the car skidded to a halt outside the hospital. It seemed only a moment or two after leaving home before he was walking in to the hospital and asking for the neurological department. He was directed to a quite, almost deserted, side section of the hospital, fronted by a large reception area.

The receptionist was a dark haired, bespectacled woman in her forties with deep green, sympathetic eyes.

"I'm Martin Clifford - my wife… she was involved in a..."

"Ah yes, Mr. Clifford…your wife is in theatre now. I'm afraid there have been some problems."

She looked up at the wall clock,

"It won't be long. The lead neurosurgeon will see you as soon as the surgical team are finished."

His heart sank. God - 'there have been some problems' - that sounded bad. He'd never been in a situation like this before and was wholly unprepared for his reaction to the crisis. He had no idea what to do, or what to say. Turning from the receptionist, he looked at the army of vacant chairs in the empty reception area and simply froze.

"Why not get a coffee Mr Clifford, machine to your right." the receptionist said gently.

Yes a coffee - something to steady his nerves and to occupy his raging emotions. That was, if he could stop his hands from shaking.

He felt in his pocket for some coins, but could find nothing. Even his tunic top was devoid of everything except the usual items he carried while on duty. His personal stuff was in the glove compartment of the patrol car, and that was miles away.

He turned back to the receptionist who, seeing him fail to find any money, held up a pound coin and proffered it in the direction of the coffee machine.

"Oh… thank you." he managed to say through thick, dry, saliva-starved lips.

"No problem. Try not to worry too much." She smiled as she handed him the coin and went back to her PC.

The remains of the coffee were nearly cold now. His back ached with the stress and tension, and the tranquil atmosphere had become overwhelmingly oppressive.

How long had he been here?

It seemed an age, but in reality it was less than fifty minutes.

Then he heard footsteps.

The man coming towards him was dressed in a full surgical gown, head cap and a facemask; the facemask having been partly loosened so it just covered the bottom of his mouth.

The surgeon strode up to him but made no effort to be polite or introductory.

"They told me you were here. You're lucky - your wife will pull through, but it was a close run thing. The next time constable, remember this, you people have to decide whether the law and your bloody duty is more important than anything else. Remember, nothing is done with impunity, or without consequences. Good day."

The overwhelming sense of relief was coupled to complete bewilderment as the gowned individual walked away.

He could find nothing to say other than a mumbled "Thank you" and remained fixed to the spot.

"You can see your wife for a few minutes in ICU if you wish Mr. Clifford."

He turned to the receptionist who beamed a smile at him.

"Did you hear the surgeon a moment ago?" he croaked, "What was that all about?"

The receptionist gave him a quizzical look "Oh, I thought you knew. When your wife was admitted our neuro-surgical registrar was faced with three different emergency procedures. He had to call in his counterpart from University

Hospital Middlehurst as a matter of life or death - your wife's life or death in fact. But it seems one of your colleagues chased and stopped him on his way here and the Middlehurst surgeon ended up in police cells. We were informed about it a little later and we reported the situation to the chief of police who ordered his release from custody. The surgeon you just met got here in a police car at breakneck speed, his own car having been impounded. Strange isn't it, your wife nearly died because the surgeon was doing in his own car what a police car did forty minutes later - but his mercy dash means he could be facing serious charges. It makes for a curious conflict of values and morality doesn't it?"

He looked down at his shoes and nodded his head, thinking back to the roadside encounter with the driver of the *Aston Martin* and realising it was self same man who had just saved his wife's life. How lucky was he that his wife had survived, but it was no thanks to him.

"Yes, I suppose it does." he whispered, deeply confused and ashamed, and not caring as he saw two uniformed men marching towards him.

He recognised their faces, and he knew why they were coming for him.

www.ingramcontent.com/pod-product-compliance
Lightning Source LLC
Chambersburg PA
CBHW051657260626
47170CB00004B/1544